The Magician's Secret

Nancy Drew

DIARIES™

The Magician's Secret

#8

CAROLYN KEENE

Aladdin

NEW YORK   LONDON   TORONTO   SYDNEY   NEW DELHI

ALADDIN

An imprint of Simon & Schuster Children's Publishing Division

1230 Avenue of the Americas, New York, NY 10020

This Aladdin paperback edition January 2015

Text copyright © 2015 by Simon & Schuster, Inc.

Cover illustrations copyright © 2015 by Erin McGuire

Also available in an Aladdin hardcover edition.

All rights reserved, including the right of reproduction in whole or in part in any form.

ALADDIN is a trademark of Simon & Schuster, Inc., and related logo is a registered trademark of Simon & Schuster, Inc.

NANCY DREW, NANCY DREW DIARIES, and related logo are trademarks of Simon & Schuster, Inc.

For information about special discounts for bulk purchases, please contact Simon & Schuster Special Sales at 1-866-506-1949 or business@simonandschuster.com.

The Simon & Schuster Speakers Bureau can bring authors to your live event. For more information or to book an event contact the Simon & Schuster Speakers Bureau at 1-866-248-3049 or visit our website at www.simonspeakers.com.

Cover designed by Karin Paprocki

Interior designed by Karina Granda

The text of this book was set in Adobe Caslon Pro.

Manufactured in the United States of America 1214 OFF

2 4 6 8 10 9 7 5 3 1

Library of Congress Control Number 2014940902

ISBN 978-1-4814-1701-3 (hc)

ISBN 978-1-4814-1700-6 (pbk)

ISBN 978-1-4814-1702-0 (eBook)

Contents

Dear Diary,

I'VE ALWAYS BEEN A LITTLE SKEPTICAL when it comes to magic. I guess the detective in me can't help wanting to know how every trick is done. But when celebrity magician Drake Lonestar decided to come to River Heights, even I was excited to see him perform. After all, it's not every day that you get to see a courthouse disappear into thin air! I just wish the evidence box for my dad's latest case hadn't disappeared too. Now I have to figure out the magic behind the mystery, before something—or someone—else vanishes!

CHAPTER ONE

A Magical Day

"I THOUGHT WE HAD PLANS," I SIGHED. "This is the third time you've canceled."

My boyfriend, Ned Nickerson, just stood in the front hallway of my house and continued typing a text message into his phone.

"Ned!"

He raised his head. "Oh, sorry. I'm in the middle of an important conversation." He took one more glance at the phone before lowering it to meet my eyes.

"You can't keep working like this. The stress isn't

good for you." I squinted, staring at his hair. "In fact, I think I see a strand of gray."

"No way!" He looked up, startled, then touched his temples.

"Just kidding," I admitted with a chuckle. "I understand that you have a million things to do. I just wish you could get some time off. Today was supposed to be fun."

"I'm sorry, Nancy. I promise I'll find time for us to hang out," he said.

"That's what you said Thursday," I replied. "And again yesterday. Now it's Saturday. You deserve the weekend off." I put my hands on my hips. "In fact, I'm going to complain to your boss. He's driving you too hard."

Ned snorted and grinned. "Good luck." He tilted his head toward my father's closed office door. "We both knew I'd be busy when your dad hired me as an intern." He paused, then added, "I just didn't realize *how* busy."

I knew what he meant. As busy as Ned was, my

dad, attorney Carson Drew, was even busier. And his latest case was taking up all his time. My dad was defending a man accused of stealing millions of dollars' worth of precious gems from a jewelry shop right in our hometown of River Heights. Dad was convinced that his client, John Smallwood, was innocent, but he couldn't prove it. Not yet, anyway.

Ned glanced down at his hand as his phone began to ring. "I really should—" He looked conflicted between answering what was obviously another important call and continuing the conversation with me.

"Don't worry." I picked up my purse from a side table near the front door. "I can go to the show by myself."

Ned drew his eyebrows together. "Show?"

"The magic show," I said, looping the purse, a new one my friend Bess had bought me, over my shoulder.

He looked at me blankly.

"Drake Lonestar . . ."

Still no sign of recognition.

"He's probably the most famous magician ever to visit River Heights," I explained. "He makes large . . .

historic . . . monuments . . . disappear. . . ." I stretched out each word, trying to jog his memory.

"Oh, right," Ned said at last. "You showed me the video of him making the Eiffel Tower vanish."

"Yes!" I was encouraged. "And the Taj Mahal. And the Sphinx in Egypt. And today, our very own River Heights courthouse."

Ned was with me now. "I'm so sorry, Nancy. I totally forgot!"

"Want to change your mind?" I held up the tickets and wiggled them in front of him. "We could sneak out the back door."

"I . . ." He paused. It was a pause full of possibility. "Maybe I could—," he began again.

Just when I thought I had convinced him, my dad's office door opened.

"Ned! Oh, good, there you are." My father walked into the foyer, past me, straight up to my boyfriend. Like Ned, he was wearing a suit, even though they were only working from our house. "You aren't answering your phone. What's the status?"

"I'm on it, Mr. Drew," Ned said, grasping his phone with tight knuckles. "The courthouse is closed today, but I called Judge Nguyen's clerk at home. She says the materials were transferred out of the judge's chambers to an evidence locker in the basement."

"It's your job to get us in to see that box." My dad tapped his toe and wrinkled his brow. "Immediately."

"I'm doing my best," Ned said. "The clerk is checking to find out if the locker can be opened later today. I'm expecting a call back any minute."

"I hope she hurries," Dad replied.

"Me too," Ned said, then turned to me. "The police gathered evidence at the crime scene. Papers and documents along with the jewelry shop's security tapes were put into crates and sealed. Then the crates were counted and cataloged at the judge's office."

"That's all perfectly normal. It's a big case," my dad put in. "The judge is keeping a personal eye on everything. Lawyers are only allowed to review the materials at certain times. When I went over there yesterday, Mr. Walton was there too." He frowned. I knew my father had worked with prosecuting attorney Ted Walton before, and he didn't trust him.

Ned continued, "The police also collected materials from Mr. Smallwood's hotel room. Along with clothes and papers, they found a locked box. No one could figure out how to open it without breaking in, and with so little time to review the materials, the box was put aside." He sighed.

I couldn't help but ask, "Any idea what's in it?"

"The police think the stolen gems are inside," Ned said.

"They don't know that for sure," my dad cut in. "The prosecution is basing the whole case on assumptions. That's why it's so important that we open the box."

"Did you ask Mr. Smallwood what's in there?" A feeling bubbled inside me—that same feeling that always happens when a mystery presents itself.

"He doesn't know, but he insists that the box isn't his," Ned replied.

"Where did it come from, then? Whose is it?" I

asked. "Does he have an explanation for why it was in his hotel room?"

Ned gave a small laugh and smiled. "Nancy Drew, Girl Detective."

I blushed but didn't back down. I'd been solving mysteries my whole life. In fact, there was already a list forming in my head. *CLUE: Unopened box. SUSPECT: John Smallwood.* My nerve endings popped with excitement as I imagined the lists growing and then diminishing as I crossed off potential suspects and sorted through clues.

My father shook his head. "I wish I had more to tell you. Whatever is in that box might be the very thing to free my client."

"But if the jewels *are* inside and it can be proven that the box belongs to Mr. Smallwood, then the box might be the very thing to put your client in jail," I reminded him.

"At this point, we need to trust that Mr. Smallwood is telling the truth; he didn't rob the store and the strange box isn't his. So"—he looked at Ned and tapped his wristwatch—"pretrial hearings start Monday. There's no time to waste. I found a locksmith who says he can open the box without damaging it; we just need access. Time to get back to it, Ned."

Ned gave me an apologetic look and, gripping his cell phone, took a step back.

My dad reached into his coat pocket. "Oh, Nancy, I almost forgot. A past client gave me two tickets to this afternoon's performance of that magic show everyone's talking about," he said, handing me an envelope. "I thought you might want to take either Bess or George."

He said that as if I would be able to take one of my two best friends without taking the other. That would *so* never happen. Dad would have realized it himself if he hadn't been so distracted.

Of course, now I had four tickets total, so I could invite them both and still have one left over for Ned. I took the envelope. "Thanks."

"Great," he said. "Have fun. I can't wait to hear all about it at dinner." He gave me a quick hug, then scooted Ned into his office.

I stood alone in the foyer. Somewhere in the bottom of my purse my cell phone buzzed. It was a text from Ned.

I'LL TRY TO MEET YOU, it said. SAVE ME A SEAT.

I smiled and quickly typed back, K. HOPE TO SEE YOU THERE.

Then I phoned George and Bess in a three-way call.

"Give me five minutes," George said after I explained what had happened. "I'll grab my stuff." I imagined her throwing a jacket and some loose cash into an old tote bag. "Just pull up out front. I'll jump in the car and then we can go get Bess."

"I need at least fifteen minutes!" Bess insisted. "And I call shotgun!"

"You had front seat last time," George argued.

"I call it again," Bess argued.

"Whatever," George replied with a groan.

George Fayne and Bess Marvin were cousins, but no one would ever guess they came from the same genetic material. Where George would show up wearing whatever she found on the floor of her room, dark hair in a tangle, with a tote bag for a purse, Bess would get dressed to the nines, make sure her blond hair was perfectly styled, and change her bag to match whatever outfit she'd selected. Fifteen minutes to Bess meant we'd be waiting for thirty.

"Bess, try to hurry," I pleaded. "I was hoping to get there a bit early. I want to look around before the show and see if I can figure out how his magic works."

"Uh-oh. Is this another case for Detective Drew? The Case of the Disappearing Courthouse?" George asked with a giggle.

"Exactly." I laughed and headed out the door.

CHAPTER TWO

The Magician

THE MAGIC SHOW WAS AT ONE P.M. RIGHT outside the River Heights courthouse. As it turned out, the seats my dad gave me were located in the same row as the ones I had bought. Bess batted her eyes and convinced an older couple to trade tickets with me so we could all sit together. She was great at getting what she wanted; the couple even smiled at her as they scooted down.

"Here." George held out Dad's ticket envelope. "We should save the seat on the aisle for Ned. That way if he shows up, he won't have to step over anyone."

On the way over it had dawned on me that it was going to be extra difficult for Ned and my dad to get into the courthouse's evidence locker today. Not only was it a Saturday, but the River Heights courthouse was the centerpiece of Drake Lonestar's show. His grand trick was to make the big historic building disappear. Even if the lawyers got permission to enter the storage area, the investigation would probably have to wait until after the performance.

So maybe Ned would be able to attend the show after all. He wasn't going to be able to do much on the case for the next few hours anyway.

I took the envelope. "Good idea. I'll sit in seat B. We'll save A for Ned." I looked over my shoulder to see if there was any sign of him. I knew I was acting obsessive, but I really hoped he would come.

There was also a different reason I was glancing around. "I'd like to check out the stage area," I said, pushing a long strand of hair off my face.

"We'll come with you." Bess smoothed her bright-green skirt and grinned at me. "The show starts in fifteen minutes. Let's see what kind of trouble you can get into until then."

I laughed. "I'm not looking for trouble."

"You never are," George replied, putting a hand on my back. "But you're a magnet for it."

"If there's trouble around, it will find you," Bess added.

"Not today," I said firmly.

"Right." George winked and Bess laughed.

As we walked to the stage area, I turned and looked toward the audience. Metal folding chairs were set in long rows. There were enough seats for about three hundred people. Employees in Lonestar T-shirts—black with a silver star on the sleeve—were ushering ticket holders to their seats.

"Wow, it's really exciting," Bess said, pointing out that there was only one entrance to the area. Curtains, ropes, and caution tape created a closed space, with the courthouse straight ahead. "I don't know why Lonestar picked River Heights, but I'm so glad he did."

"He threw a dart at a US map and then came to the

place that it landed on," George said. "It just happened to be River Heights."

Bess looked at her. "How on earth did you know that?"

"When Nancy said her dad had the extra seats, I checked him out online." George shrugged as if she wondered why Bess hadn't thought to do the same.

"You amaze me," Bess said, shaking her head.

A banging sound made us all swing around.

George pointed. "Hey, look!"

There was a commotion near the back of the audience. At the left side of the entryway, a man had jumped the rope boundary. He was shouting, "Drake! You're the best!" In literally seconds, the Lonestar staff had stopped him and were escorting him outside.

I took a sharp breath and quickly scanned the area. "Security sure is tight," I noted. Big signs had warned: NO CAMERAS OR RECORDING DEVICES. We'd had to leave our smartphones at a check-in booth. In addition to Lonestar's own security team, the local police were out in force.

Above us, two helicopters hovered in the distance. The blades hummed in the light spring breeze. I pointed them out to Bess and George.

"Those are military helicopters," George remarked. Along with computers, her obsession was anything mechanical. She knew a lot about all kinds of hardware. "I think the models were retired. Must be more of the magician's private security." She made a clicking sound with her tongue. "Interesting."

I'd never seen a show like this, but I wondered if the security and helicopters were there to protect skeptics from ruining the illusion. I assumed I wasn't the only one there who was eager to figure out how the trick worked.

I turned toward the stage. It was the same standard rented raised platform the town used for outdoor concerts, and it had been set up near the bottom of the courthouse steps. Several thick, billowy velvet curtains framed the stage, and spotlights dotted the makeshift ceiling.

"Come on," I said to my friends. "Let's check it out."

"Don't get too close," George said, then leaned in and warned, "You don't want to get kicked out because you were snooping."

"We aren't snooping," I countered. "We're just surveying the scene!"

As I said that, I could feel the eyes of a Lonestar employee watching our every move. Glancing over my shoulder, I spotted a security guard with thinning, gray-speckled brown hair and very big arm muscles standing under a tree. He winked at me, not in a bad way, but in a way that let me know he was doing his job.

I gave him a tiny smile and looked away.

Bess pulled my arm and we moved to the side of the stage, where a small set of steps led to a thick, black curtain.

I guess Bess and George could sense my inner detective getting into gear, because they both shook their heads, but I put my finger to my lips, checked to make sure the burly security guard wasn't looking our way, and darted up the steps. I knew it probably wasn't the smartest move, but I was dying to know what was back there. And Bess and George must have felt the same, because they followed me. I parted the curtain panels, and the three of us found ourselves in the stage's wings.

The stage setup was simple: a table sat in the middle with black top hat—the old-fashioned kind magicians usually drew a rabbit from—sitting on it. I have to admit, I was surprised the stage was so bare. I don't know what I expected, but at least a few props or something.

"Magic baffles me," I said. "It takes so much preparation to pull off a single trick." I seriously had no idea how Drake Lonestar was going to make the huge, solid courthouse disappear, and looking around the stage certainly gave me no clues.

Suddenly loud orchestral music blared from the speakers, and the stage curtains slowly pulled back. A murmur rose from the audience, who seemed to be scrambling back to their seats.

"Wait!" George hissed. "Is that smoke? The show isn't supposed to start yet."

Sure enough, smoke had started emanating from the stage. I squinted, trying to make out what was happening.

Bess glanced at her watch. "It's still ten minutes to showtime. Maybe he likes to get things started early?"

Just then the hat levitated a few inches off the table, hovering in midair for about a minute before settling down again.

Screams and whistles, as well as scattered applause, could be heard from the audience, and the curtain closed once again.

"Whoa! Did you guys see that?" George exclaimed. "I wonder if the hat was connected by wires."

"We sometimes like to give our audience a little preshow teaser." A tall and very physically fit man appeared, seemingly from nowhere. He was about my dad's age, had long, dark, curly hair, and was wearing sunglasses that were so dark I couldn't see his eyes. He held out his hand. "I'm Drake Lonestar."

"I'm Nancy," I said, and quickly introduced Bess and George too.

"It's no fair snooping around before the show," he said with a chuckle. "This trick demands an audience that's willing to believe in the illusion."

"Oh—um, I—," I stuttered. "We weren't snooping. . . ."

Bess coughed.

"We're just surveying the scene," George said as she elbowed me in the ribs and chuckled.

I quickly changed the subject. "I've seen your magic on TV. Very impressive. Of course, I can't help but wonder how you make things disappear."

"You'll see for yourself soon enough," Drake Lonestar said. "Be patient. Are you willing to believe, even for a moment, that what I am about to do is real?"

"I . . ." I stalled. If I had to admit the truth, then the answer was no. I liked understanding what really happened behind the curtain. Was I willing to let go of the detective in me, just for an hour?

"I'll try to sit back and enjoy the show," I finally answered.

"That's all I can ask," Lonestar said. And with a

wave of his hand, he produced three roses out of thin air. He gave one to Bess, one to George, and one to me.

"Hugo will take you back to your seats."

Hugo turned out to be the beefy guard who'd winked at me earlier. He surprised me when he put a hand on my back. I jumped, and Lonestar laughed.

"Hugo LaBlanca has been on my staff for twenty years. If I disappeared right now, I'd trust him to take over the show." Lonestar snapped his fingers, and I half expected him to actually disappear, but he didn't.

For his part, while Lonestar was joking around, Hugo showed no response. He touched my elbow, which made me jump again, and a moment later escorted us away, with no room for any further snooping . . . or surveying.

We hadn't gotten far when Drake Lonestar called out to me, "Nancy Drew."

I turned.

Wait a minute. Drake Lonestar had just called me by my last name, but I was positive I hadn't told him anything other than "Nancy" when we'd first met.

"Don't forget." He took off his sunglasses and stared at me with the greenest cat eyes I had ever seen. "Magic is a mystery that doesn't need solving."

His words echoed in my ears as Hugo led us back into the audience.

CHAPTER THREE

~

Onstage

I SAT DOWN IN SEAT B AND TWISTED THE rose stem. The blossom was closed, the petals waiting to open and reveal the fragrance inside.

"Did you hear what he said?" I asked my friends. "Mystery? Somehow he knows who I am."

George rolled her eyes and muttered, "I wouldn't take anything that guy says seriously, Nancy. He was so arrogant. Instead let's try to figure out how the trick is done."

"I liked him," Bess cut in. She ran the rose across her cheek. "He's charming."

"Blech." George rolled her eyes. "You'd think any guy who gave you flowers was charming."

"Maybe," Bess admitted. "But tell me, George— how did he know there were three of us? He would have needed to have the roses with him when he first approached."

"He saw us outside the curtain," George said, shrugging. "Not so tricky."

Bess was clearly willing to let the magic slide over and impress her. George, not so much.

On this I was more like George, but I'd promised Lonestar I'd try to be more like Bess. Letting my mind go blank was harder than I had ever imagined, and I had to chase away any thoughts that the rose was in his sleeve or that he'd had an accomplice or that he'd distracted us with Hugo. I was fighting against my own busy brain.

I was grateful when the show's music started again and the curtains parted.

With a puff of smoke and a flash of lights, Drake Lonestar appeared, seemingly from nowhere, up on the stage.

He waved a hand and a screen appeared behind him. On the screen was a short video. I couldn't help myself. I flipped my head around to look for a projector. I didn't see one, but that didn't mean anything. I wasn't privy to the latest, most advanced technology; that was George's domain.

Poof.

A flash of smoke and Lonestar levitated above the stage, floating high over the screen.

"Wires," George whispered to me, though I didn't see any. He hovered while the screen lit up with his name and logo.

The video was entertaining. It showed clips from Lonestar's other tricks around the globe. He'd made more buildings disappear than just the ones I'd told Ned about. There was a bank in Zurich, a hotel in South Africa, and even a large tower in Hong Kong. The video did also, in fact, show him throwing a dart at a US map and picking River Heights. And it showed a three-dimensional model of our courthouse building.

When the screen disappeared with a flash of light, Lonestar was no longer airborne. Now he stood on the stage flanked by two stunning models in miniskirts and the Lonestar T-shirts we'd seen earlier.

Bess leaned past George and whispered, "I have that same skirt at home. It's the newest from Gritty Grand, the Australian designer. She's a rising superstar."

George pointed at a camera and crew that were now standing at the back of the audience. "Can't hurt to have your clothes on display at a popular show," she said. "Great exposure."

I nodded, feeling slightly disappointed that I hadn't noticed the recording crew. Of course the show was being taped, just like all of Drake's other illusions. We could probably revisit the whole performance on the Internet later this week.

"My friends!" Drake Lonestar raised his hands, and as he did, the back of the stage slowly disappeared into the ground so that the courthouse behind it was clearly visible to the audience. The historic building had been built about two hundred years earlier, with wide cement stairs ascending to carved oak doors. Beautiful stained-glass windows dotted the front, and ferocious stone gargoyles guarded the entry. A tower at the top overlooked the grassy stage area.

All the civic work of River Heights took place inside that building, from criminal trials to council meetings to government document processing. A branch of the police department and some jail holding cells were there too. During the week the place was busy, but on weekends it was closed to the public.

Unless you convince a clerk to call a judge and let you in, I thought, remembering Ned and my father.

I shook my head and focused on the show. Drake Lonestar's assistants raised a large circular object that looked like a Hula-Hoop. The perspective of the hoop made us all focus on the courthouse, which from my angle fit neatly inside its round-edged boundaries. I reasoned that he'd worked out the seating so that the courthouse was framed inside the circle from every chair.

"In a moment," Drake announced in a big, booming voice, "the building you see in front of you will cease to exist." The audience applauded. He paused. "For the skeptics among you, I offer this."

With a finger snap, a barrel appeared on the stage in front of him. It was one of those thin wire mesh tumblers that lottery numbers or bingo letters are picked from. Inside were slips of paper.

He took the side handle and rotated the barrel.

"One lucky member of the audience will join me onstage." He laughed. "The best view in the house."

Drake spun the barrel a few more times, then pulled out a slip of paper. With another finger snap, the tumbler disappeared into smoke. He looked at the number. Then he looked at me.

"The lucky person for today's show is . . ." There was no drumroll. Only silence. "Row five. Seat B."

"Hey! That's your seat, Nancy." Bess put her arm around me and gave me a big hug. "Congratulations!"

I didn't move. There was something funny going on. Out of everyone in the audience, he'd picked my seat. My number. Was it magic? Fate? Or something else?

Then I realized that I wasn't supposed to be in that particular seat. It was one of the tickets my dad had given me. And I had only sat there because George wanted me to be near Ned. I'd been the one to determine that if he showed up, he'd take the aisle.

"It has to be a coincidence," I told myself as Hugo arrived to usher me up the steps to the stage.

The magician held out his hand to escort me to a folding chair that he'd placed to the side. Sitting there, I'd have a clear view of the courthouse. I noticed there were small silver pieces of tape that marked where the chair was placed. This stunt had obviously been planned in advance.

I tried to tell myself that there was no way it was planned for *me*. I was being paranoid. He didn't know I was coming to the show or which seats I had.

But then again, there was the fact that he knew my name and hinted at my mystery-solving background. Something strange was going on, but what?

"Meet Nancy Drew!" he announced, pulling the chair back and settling me into it as if we were at a fine restaurant.

I sat down, not sure what else I could do.

Drake moved to the center of the stage, where his assistants rejoined him. They held up the Hula-Hoop. From my view, the courthouse filled every inch of the circle.

"The courthouse is closed today," Lonestar said. "We checked that the doors are locked. We even invited all courthouse employees to attend the performance." He asked anyone who worked at the courthouse to stand. "Our greatest civil service workers," he boomed. "The importance of justice can never be understated."

While Drake told a story about how he had been a troubled kid whose life was changed by magic, I let my eyes turn away to peek out at George and Bess. To my surprise, Ned had arrived.

He was sitting in the seat I'd saved for him. Row 5, seat A. Seeing Ned made me more determined than ever to enjoy the show. Like the rest of the audience, I stared through the hoop at the court-house building.

"An illusion demands that the audience participate fully," Lonestar said as he did a little sleight of hand. It was similar to when he'd made the roses appear, but this time a bright-red silk square fluttered from his palm.

He raised the silk. The material fully covered the hoop, blocking the audience's view of the building beyond.

And that was it. We couldn't see the courthouse.

Without another word, he lowered the scarf.

The courthouse was gone.

The crowd went wild.

Drake looked at me and smiled. "Nancy?" he asked. "Do you see the courthouse?"

I shook my head.

"The audience can't hear you . . . ," he prodded.

"No," I said loudly. "It's gone."

Drake instructed the assistants to drop the hoop. Even without the frame of perspective, the building was—as far as my eyes could tell—gone.

The buzz of the helicopters that we'd heard when we first arrived grew louder.

"Oh no!" Drake exclaimed as the copters got close enough that we could feel the breeze from their whirling blades. "They'll hit the building!" He was joking, of course, and laughed as two helicopters flew through the space where the building had stood. If the courthouse had been there, they'd have crashed into it.

I closed my eyes, blinked hard, and reopened them. There was a broad open area where the courthouse used to stand.

The helicopters circled around and soared through the spot again before Lonestar raised the hoop, instructing the audience to look inside as he held up the scarf.

A moment later, he dropped both the cloth and the hoop.

The courthouse was back.

The audience roared with applause. Everyone, including me, stood for an ovation. I flicked my eyes to the crowd and saw Bess and Ned cheering. George was standing at her seat, but she had her hands on her hips. I could see by the scrunched-up look on her face that she was trying desperately to figure out what she'd seen and how it worked.

Drake Lonestar took his bow and, with a puff of smoke, disappeared from the stage. Then he reappeared, laughing. "I forgot something important," he joked, taking the arms of his two assistants. "I can't leave these ladies behind!" An instant later the three of them were gone.

I was left standing alone on the stage. I looked for Hugo to come and walk me back to my seat, but he was over to the side, talking to the chief of the River Heights police force.

The show was over. There'd be no more illusion or fanfare. I even had to walk myself off the stage to meet my friends and Ned.

"I'm headed back to your dad's office," Ned said, kissing my cheek before taking off. "This was fun. But are you sure you can you handle all this?" He looked around, gesturing to the crowd that had gathered around us. There were quite a few people clamoring for my attention, shouting questions about Lonestar and the trick.

"We've got her covered," George said.

I answered whatever questions I could, but the truth was, I'd seen the same as anyone in the audience. There was no great secret I could reveal.

About half an hour later, Bess, George, and I managed to get our phones from the check-in desk and were headed to our cars.

"Whew," Bess sighed. "Want to go to the mall? There are some shoes that I want both your opinions on."

"I'm free," I said.

"Not like I have anything better to do," George said. "Though I wish I did." She exhaled heavily. Shopping wasn't her thing.

I had just opened the car door when two officers rushed toward us.

"Not so fast," one of them said, putting up a hand. "We have a few questions for you, Ms. Drew."

"You were seen talking to Drake Lonestar before the show," the other officer said.

"Yes." I shrugged. "I was walking around and he approached me." My sleuthing senses tingled. "What's going on?"

"You're our key witness," the first officer said. "An important box of evidence was being held in a basement storage locker of the courthouse."

"When the courthouse disappeared, so did the box," the other officer continued. "It's gone."

CHAPTER FOUR

❧

Gone Missing

LATER THAT AFTERNOON MY FATHER'S WISH was finally granted. He *was* inside the courthouse.

But then again, so were most of the River Heights police force, prosecutor Ted Walton, Hugo, Lonestar's two assistants, the judge's clerk, George, Bess, Ned, and me. We all stood together, crammed inside the small storage locker where the Smallwood case evidence was stored.

Ted Walton held a clipboard and was flipping through the attached pages. "Where was the courthouse security guard?" he asked a tall, thin police officer whose name tag read COLLINS.

"There was no guard on duty, since the building is officially closed today," Officer Collins replied. "It's highly unusual that anything is stolen from the storage lockers." He punctuated that by adding, "It's *never* happened before."

The stunned clerk said, "All employees were outside watching the show the entire time." She sighed. "Wait until Judge Nguyen hears what happened," she moaned. "I don't want to be the one to tell her."

"She knows," my dad said. "I called her." He put a hand on the clerk's shoulder. "She understands that it's not your fault the box disappeared."

A young police officer said, "When River Heights agreed to host Drake Lonestar's show, the mayor made sure that no court employees would come in that weekend. Not even janitorial staff. He also agreed to turn off all surveillance cameras for an hour to protect the integrity of the trick. There didn't seem to be a risk of anything like this. Plus, it was great publicity for River Heights." Her shoulders slumped.

Mr. Walton was a burly man with a hot temper. "Well, the mayor was wrong," he shouted with a red, sweaty face. "Because we *do* have a problem!" His voice echoed off the cement walls. "A big problem."

The locker was about the size of a small bathroom. The boxes of evidence from the Smallwood case were marked and set against the back walls. There were only three of them.

"The obvious conclusion is that Drake Lonestar removed the mystery box from the courthouse locker during the show," Mr. Walton continued in a calmer tone. "Find the magician, find the box. And I am certain you will discover that inside the box are the gems, which Mr. Smallwood stole." He added, "In fact, I'll bet money on it that Smallwood and Lonestar are in this together."

"Now wait a minute." My dad faced Mr. Walton. "You have no proof of any of that. You can't go around stating your opinions as if they were facts. That's not how justice works. Mr. Smallwood is innocent until proven guilty. So far we have no evidence that links him to the box, the gems, or to Drake Lonestar."

Mr. Walton was shorter than my dad but didn't seem to be intimidated. He rushed forward until the two men were toe-to-toe and bellowed, "Your client is a thief! No doubt about it."

"Prove it in court!" Dad countered.

They began to argue.

Hugo stepped between them.

An impressive thing about Hugo was the quiet way he asserted himself. He didn't have to say much—or in this situation anything at all—to show that he was in control. Both my dad and Mr. Walton retreated immediately, and the argument ended.

I turned to Ned. We hadn't had time to talk about what was going on, and I was suddenly curious as to how he'd gotten into the magic show at all. I still had his ticket in my purse, and security at the magic show had been as tight as a vault.

Ned leaned over and whispered to me, "Mr. Walton

is going crazy because besides whatever is in that missing box, the only real evidence he has against Smallwood are the store's security tapes. And those only show that Mr. Smallwood was the last man in the jewelry shop on the night it was robbed." He took my hand and led me out of the locker so we could have a minute alone. "If he hadn't been previously convicted of burglary, I don't think he'd be a suspect at all."

I raised my eyebrows.

"As it is, he got out of prison last month after serving a year for armed robbery," Ned continued.

"What did he steal?" I asked.

"Diamonds," Ned replied. "Two millions dollars' worth of them from a shop in Switzerland."

"Really?" I inhaled sharply. "What was missing from the shop here?"

"Emeralds." Ned pinched his lips together and wrinkled his forehead. "And rubies."

"No diamonds?" I considered that.

"No. It's something in your dad's favor for the defense. Your dad might be able to say that

Mr. Smallwood was only interested in diamonds, so he couldn't possibly be the thief." He quickly added, "Plus, Smallwood just got out of prison. Why would he want to risk going back there?"

"Is he the only suspect in the burglary?" I asked.

"So far." Ned frowned. He pointed at the storage locker. "That's why they took everything from his hotel room. He'd been staying there a week and was supposed to leave tomorrow. He's not being held in jail, but he's not allowed to leave town yet either. So he's staying with a friend in River Heights."

I nodded. The police couldn't keep Mr. Smallwood in town indefinitely. They were going to have to either file charges against him or let him leave River Heights.

Ned motioned toward the crates against the wall. "Every scrap of paper from Smallwood's trash, the book he was reading, even his toothbrush is in one of those boxes. They are going to investigate him down to the hairs on his head."

We moved back to where the police were now

showing Mr. Walton the lock to the storage room. My dad was hanging at the back of the group.

"There's no sign of forced entry," Officer Collins was saying. "And Judge Nguyen has the only key."

As I got closer, my father raised his shoulder at me, just a tiny bit, and tilted his head. It was his way of asking me to move in closer. I could tell that he wanted me to take a look around, so I gave him the smallest of nods.

Then, with a silent signal of my own, I brought in George. If anyone could figure out how that locker had been opened, she was the one.

George had been standing with Bess, chatting with Hugo and the two assistants. I had no doubt Bess was asking about their designer skirts. The speed with which George came over to me confirmed it. Skirts were definitely not a topic she enjoyed. All I had to do was look at her, then glance at the locker, and she came rushing across the room.

"You saved me," George said gratefully. "Apparently Hugo is dating that designer . . . Gritty Grand." She made a face. "Who names a child that?"

As George stepped away to check out the storage room lock, a second officer, a woman whose name tag read FERNANDEZ, approached me.

"Got a minute, Nancy?" she asked. Her dark hair was pulled back in a dancer's tight bun.

"Sure," I said. I was confident that George would find out anything I might want to know about the lock, and Bess was probably gathering important information by speaking to Lonestar's staff.

"We suspect that Drake Lonestar had something to do with the box's disappearance," Officer Fernandez told me. "Did you see anything onstage that might have indicated he was up to no good?"

"Up to no good?" I repeated. "No."

"You didn't see him disappear during the trick or stash something or . . ." She fumbled for the right question before settling on a direct approach. "In your opinion, is there any chance he slipped away during the trick, snuck into the courthouse, and stole the box?"

I considered the question. Lonestar had told me

not to think too much about how the trick worked, so I intentionally hadn't concentrated on details. As far as I could remember, he was onstage the whole time. He did disappear at the end, but only for a second, and then he disappeared again with his assistants. Would that have been enough time to get into the courthouse and take a box? I didn't think so, but in this world of magic, nothing seemed certain.

"No," I admitted, then asked Officer Fernandez a question of my own. "Have you talked to Mr. Lonestar?"

"We would if we could find him," she said. "It seems that the magician has disappeared."

"No one has seen him since the show?" I asked, glancing over at Bess with Lonestar's staff. They were all laughing at something Bess had said.

"No," the officer reported. "When he vanished from the stage that last time, he never reappeared. We have a team of officers searching River Heights. They'll track him down."

"Can you excuse me for a moment?" I asked. I hurried over to Lonestar's assistants.

"Hi," I said, noticing that they weren't much older than me.

Bess introduced us. "This is Ayela." She indicated the one on her right. "And Ariana." The other one smiled. "They're twins. And their aunt is fashion designer Gritty Grand."

"Ah." If Hugo was dating Gritty, it stood to reason that he would hire her nieces as Lonestar's helpers. I shook hands with each of them, then asked, "So, where is Mr. Lonestar?"

They didn't know.

"But you performed the last trick with him," I said. "You vanished together from the stage."

"Oh, we can't reveal how it's done," Ayela said.

"We'd be fired," Ariana added.

"I don't need to know how it's done," I said, though I *was* curious. "I just wondered where Lonestar went afterward."

"The police already asked them," Hugo told me. "They don't know."

He moved toward me in a way that almost

seemed threatening. I stepped back to give myself some space from the burly bodyguard and looked to Ayela and Ariana. "Where did you reappear?"

Ayela and Hugo exchanged glances before she replied, "In the dressing-room tent."

"But Drake wasn't with us," Ariana said. "I guess you could say he dropped us off." She smiled.

"You don't know where he went?" I asked.

"No," they said at the same time.

"Who can ever guess what that man is up to? Drake Lonestar's got kangaroos loose in the top paddock," Ayela said with a giggle.

I decided to give the girls a rest. I wouldn't get anywhere by badgering them with the same question over and over.

The facts were clear:

• Drake Lonestar was missing.
• A box that had been in evidence storage was missing.
• More than a million dollars' worth of gems were missing.

I was standing in the middle of a major mystery with a lot of unanswered questions. Still, one question loomed over the entire scene, bigger than the rest: What did any of this have to do with my dad's client, John Smallwood?

~∾∾~

CHAPTER FIVE

No
Coincidence

A HALF HOUR LATER THE SAME CROWD
from the basement had moved to just outside the
courthouse. Officer Fernandez continued to question
Lonestar's staff, while the rest of the police investi-
gated the evidence locker. The sun was bright in the
sky. Bess absentmindedly fanned herself with one of
Lonestar's programs.

"Whew, it sure warmed up out here," Hugo muttered, removing his jacket. As he swung his coat
over his arm, a stack of small white cards fell out of
the pocket.

He leaped forward to pick them up, but Officer Fernandez stopped him.

"Can that wait? I have a question for you," she said, putting her hand on his chest.

His eyes went to the cards. "Give me one minute. I need to—"

"Mr. LaBlanca, please. This is important," she said firmly.

My curiosity was piqued. What was on those cards? And why did he need to gather them so badly? I kneeled down to pick up the cards myself, but before I could find out what was on them, Bess dropped to her knees next to me.

"Nancy," she whispered. "I've got something to tell you."

Bess picked up a few white cards. "While I was speaking to Ariana and Ayela, I suddenly remembered an article I read recently about Gritty Grand. If the report is accurate, she's broke. According to a rival designer, her company is shutting down."

"Do you think it's true?" I asked.

"Probably. Bad news often is," Bess said. "The thing is that Gritty Grand's response to the report was that this rival designer 'has kangaroos loose in the top paddock.' I thought it was such a strange thing to say that I remembered it."

"I'm guessing it's simply Australian slang," I suggested. "It's possible that it's just one of those phrases everyone says, like 'she's got a screw loose.'"

"I'm not sure." Bess pinched her lips together. "I mean, we are looking for a jewel thief, and there's the possibility that Gritty Grand, who we've now connected to Drake Lonestar through her boyfriend and nieces, might be broke."

The wheels started turning in my head. "I get what you're saying," I told Bess. "If she needed money to save her business, she might be interested in gems. That could be the connection we need to attach Lonestar to Smallwood."

"While you're thinking about that," Bess said, "I have something else for you to consider."

She handed me two of the cards we'd picked up from

the floor. "They all say 5A on one side and 5B on the other," Bess pointed out.

They were the white cards from the barrel that Lonestar had used to choose his onstage guest! Me.

So it wasn't a coincidence that I was onstage for the performance. My dad had given me two tickets: seats 5A and 5B. Whichever seat I chose, I'd have been selected.

The moment Hugo and Officer Fernandez ended their conversation, I leaped forward.

"Hugo," I said, thrusting out my hands filled with the white cards. "Care to explain?"

He laughed as he took them from my hands and tossed them into a nearby trash can. There was distinct humor in his eyes and a smile on his face.

"It was part of the marketing plan," Hugo explained easily. "Drake heard about you, Nancy Drew. You're famous around here."

I wrinkled my nose. Sure, I'd solved a few mysteries, but I would never consider myself famous. Not like Drake Lonestar. He had fans screaming his name, jumping fences for him, and begging for autographs. I had a couple of articles in the local paper. There was no comparison.

"Drake decided he wanted you onstage. So he sent the tickets to your dad under the name of a past client that he'd read about in the news."

"How did you know my father wouldn't give them to our housekeeper, or take someone else himself?"

"It was a risk," Hugo admitted. "But Drake's a magician, Nancy. He'd have found a way to get you to the show, and anywhere you'd have sat, he would have picked you."

I nodded.

"Drake figured that it would be much more impressive to have a known detective onstage, watching the trick with eagle eyes." He added, "He also made sure that the ticket desk let your boyfriend in when he showed up. Just another pair of eyes confirming the wonder created by Drake Lonestar."

My conversation with Hugo answered the question of how Ned got to his seat without a ticket. And it answered how my dad got tickets to the show. The problem was, there were so many questions still left unanswered.

CHAPTER SIX

A Midnight Chat

"HEY, GEORGE," I HISSED. "YOU AWAKE?"

It was late at night, and I was standing outside my friend's bedroom window after having given up on sleep. All the excitement of the day had made my head feel full, and I figured that if George could clear up a couple of important things, maybe I'd be able to rest.

"George!" I banged my knuckles on the glass pane.

"Go away, Nancy!"

That wasn't George. It was Bess. I'd forgotten she was sleeping at her cousin's house.

I could see Bess roll over and put her pillow over her head.

"Go back to sleep, Bess." George sat up. "I'll take care of the intruder." She opened the window. "Come on in," she said, moving aside and giving me space to crawl through the frame.

"Thanks," I said.

"I wasn't sleeping anyway," George admitted. She tipped her head toward her bed, and I could see a faint blue glow under the covers.

"Late night Internet research?" I asked with a grin.

"You know it." She glanced at Bess. "Had to be quiet, though . . . don't want to disturb the *princess*."

"I heard that," Bess grunted from the bed next to George's. "The princess needs her beauty sleep. Now *shhhhh*." She turned her back to us.

I whispered to George, "This case is making me crazy. I don't see a connection between Smallwood and Lonestar." I sat on the edge of George's bed. "I mean, we could guess that Lonestar hired Smallwood to steal the gems for Hugo to give to the nieces to give to Gritty Grand, but that seems like a long and winding chain of relationships. There's no evidence to prove any of that."

"I hear you," George agreed. "We need some hard facts." She turned her computer screen to face me.

"Ack, the light!" Bess whimpered from the other bed. "It's coming into my head through the back of my skull."

"Oh, good grief," George moaned. She packed up the computer and led me into the bathroom. She sat on the closed toilet lid. I shut the door so we wouldn't bug Bess anymore and sat on the edge of the bathtub.

"I wasn't searching for connections between the suspects," George told me, typing on her laptop. "I was thinking more about the trick." She showed me a site and scrolled down the page. "I was right about the helicopters. They are an old military model that's been retired. Anyone can hire them for air shows . . . or magic shows."

"Do you think the helicopters have a connection to the missing box?" I asked.

"No," George admitted. "But I am obsessed with figuring out how the trick worked. Right now I have two theories: One is that the audience was hypnotized, and the other is that somehow we were still watching a video even after Lonestar dropped the hoop. So we weren't seeing the actual building, but a screen with doctored images of the empty space. The helicopters were there to throw us off."

"I guess both are possible." A big part of me wanted to have George figure it out, but Lonestar's voice in my head told me to let it be. As much as I wanted to ask more about her theories, especially the mass hypnosis, I let it drop.

Instead I asked George, "Do you have any idea how the locker was opened in the courthouse? Or when? We need to know if Lonestar had enough time during the trick to get into the evidence locker and take that box."

"I've been thinking about that, too," she told me. "There are many different kinds of magic, but most magicians specialize in one or two and hone their craft.

From everything I've read about Lonestar, he's what one would call an illusionist. That means he does big, showy tricks that seem impossible, like cutting people in half, levitating, and making things disappear."

George had done her homework. She went on, "Illusions take a lot of planning. Not that this is set in stone, but if an illusionist was the one to open the lock, he'd probably have manipulated it earlier—like sawed off part of the barrel or wedged something inside to prevent it from really closing all the way." She bit a fingernail thoughtfully.

"And?" I prodded.

"When I looked at the lock, nothing seemed altered. I looked for markings, like scratches from picking tools; I searched the floor for rubber bands or cork or gum that might have held the locking mechanism open. Nothing."

"So what's your verdict?" I asked.

George leaned back on the toilet tank and closed her eyes. "Officer Fernandez told me that the police have two theories. Either someone had keys to the evidence locker and stole that box or an accomplice let the thief into the locker while the show was going on. I think there is another possibility. . . ."

"Magic?" I asked.

"Yes. But not Lonestar's kind of magic. He's a showy guy with big costumes and setups. I just don't see this as his kind of trick." She went on. "This is essentially an escape. Someone opened the lock and then escaped from the sealed evidence room with the box. When I think about it like that, it fits in with the kind of magic that's about picking locks and getting out of tight spaces, which is called escapism. Harry Houdini was the most famous escape artist. He once did a trick where he was locked in a jail cell and managed to get out in less than twenty minutes."

"That's amazing!" I was going to have to look up that one later. I asked George, "So, from everything you know about magic, it sounds like you think Drake Lonestar isn't our number one suspect."

"I've searched the Internet to see if he's ever done any escapes from boxes or secure rooms, but can't find anything. He might know how to do some of those tricks, but from everything I can see, he doesn't. He's all illusion all the time." George shook her head. "From a magic point of view, he simply doesn't make sense."

I slipped down into the empty bathtub and put my head against the cool tile wall. It seemed like we'd hit a dead end. Usually I had a list of suspects and clues. But this case was filled with suspects without clues and clues without suspects.

What I did have was a previously convicted thief who denied he stole anything, missing gems, the cast of a magic show, a locked door, and a mysterious box that had disappeared—all pieces of a puzzle that didn't fit together.

"What do we do next?" George asked me.

"I don't—," I started.

"You two are so loud!" Bess stomped into the bathroom. "I'll tell you what we do next. John Smallwood was staying at a hotel for the week, right? The Drake Lonestar magic show team has been here a week too.

They're also at a hotel. That might be a place to start searching for connections."

George's face lit up. "You're right! There aren't that many hotels in town. It's possible they're staying in the same place."

So we weren't going to figure out how Drake Lonestar made the courthouse disappear, and we weren't going to figure out how the box vanished from the evidence locker, but we were back on track with my initial burning question: Was Smallwood in any way connected to Lonestar?

~❦~

CHAPTER SEVEN

Connecting the Dots

IT WAS STILL DARK, BUT THE SUN WAS slowly rising when Bess, George, and I piled into my car.

"I want the last doughnut," Bess complained from the backseat.

"No way," George countered. "You already had two."

It had been my idea to quickly stop for coffee and doughnuts at the all-night diner. Thing was, I only wanted one glazed, and the employee insisted that a half dozen was cheaper. I shouldn't have given in to the pressure. Or else, I should have just eaten the last one and prevented this whole heated discussion.

"Going to check hotel registers was my idea," Bess said. "That should be enough for extra chocolate cream privileges."

"I was up all night learning about magicians," George said. "That should be my ticket to the treat."

"I was up too," Bess argued. "Because you're so noisy!"

They kept at it until we reached the nicest hotel in town, the Towering Heights Resort. I'd texted Ned to find out where Smallwood had been staying. This was it. I pulled into a parking spot.

Now, to see who else might have stayed there.

It only took a minute to find out that the magician and his crew weren't registered.

"Rats," I muttered as we drove to the second-nicest hotel in town. Then the third. And fourth.

The sun was high in the sky when we reached the last option on our list: a low-budget hotel on the outskirts of town. It was called the Riverview, though it was so far from the river there was no way the name was true. The Highway Traffic View Hotel just didn't sound as nice, I supposed.

It was my turn to run in and ask the front desk about our missing magician.

"Nancy? What are you doing here?"

I whirled around to find Hugo sitting at a small table in the lobby, reading the newspaper and drinking a cup of coffee from the local River Run Coffee Shop.

"I—" I wasn't sure what to tell Hugo. After all, he worked for Lonestar. What would he do to protect his boss from going to jail?

"We're supposed to start tearing down the set today, but the police still can't find Drake," Hugo told me.

"I assumed he'd be here at the hotel with you," I said, watching as Hugo swirled the coffee in his cup.

"He was. But now he's not," Hugo said. "Celebrity admirers can get really aggressive when they want to meet their idol," he explained. "The first night we were here, a man climbed in through Drake's hotel window. I had to chase the guy down the street. Drake always registers at hotels under phony names to avoid fans, but this one was more persistent than most and followed us back after rehearsal."

Hmm . . . So he might have been staying under a different name at one of the hotels we'd already visited.

"So where is Drake now?" I asked.

"I don't know," Hugo said, staring past my left shoulder.

I turned and saw Ayela and Ariana entering the lobby. As they got in line for the vending machine, they waved at Hugo, who grinned back.

He turned back to me. "Drake moved after that first night. He changed hotels, picked a fake name to register under, and got himself to rehearsals."

"But you're his bodyguard! You let him do that without protection?" I asked.

"The truly devoted fans know me by now; a lot of them follow me if they think I'm with him, so we often separate. He goes off the grid. No e-mail. No cell phones. It's not a big deal. Drake knows to meet me at the train station on Tuesday."

"That's when you're leaving?" I asked. "Two days from now?"

"Magic is really draining, so Drake likes a few days

of rest before traveling to the next show," Hugo said. "But like I told Officer Fernandez, I fully expect that he'll be at the train station Tuesday."

"Hugo!" Ariana and Ayela ran toward us.

"Nancy!" Bess and George called my name as they entered the hotel.

"The radio!" they cried at the same time as Ariana and Ayela yelled, "The radio!" Apparently the four of them had been listening to the same station.

Hugo and I rushed to the closest TV set, in the hotel bar. A handcuffed Drake Lonestar was on the screen, flanked by Officer Fernandez on his left and Officer Collins on his right.

Beyond them were screaming fans, desperate to get a glimpse of the magician. There were countless women carrying signs that said I LOVE YOU and MARRY ME! A guy was standing on the courthouse steps selling Drake Lonestar T-shirts. The crowd was chanting his name.

Even with all the chaos surrounding him, we clearly could hear Drake shout, "I'd rather spend a lifetime in prison than reveal how my magic is done!"

CHAPTER EIGHT

❧

Jail Time

I'D NEVER DRIVEN SO FAST IN MY LIFE.

When Bess, George, and I arrived at the courthouse, Drake Lonestar was already inside—getting booked, I presumed, but I hadn't a clue under what charge.

The courthouse was usually closed on Sunday, just like Saturday, but today, like yesterday, it was bustling.

Reporters were milling around, waiting for a story. My dad was off to the side with Ned. Even at a distance, I could see that Ned's hair was standing up and his suit, the same one he'd worn the day before, was rumpled. He'd clearly been working all night.

Hugo, with Gritty Grand's nieces in tow, pulled his rental car into the space next to mine, and all six of us ran across the parking lot together. I raced up to Ned.

"I wondered when you'd show up," he said, kissing me hello on the cheek. "News travels fast in River Heights."

"I saw the arrest on TV."

He nodded. "But the news only reported that Lonestar was picked up. An hour ago John Smallwood was also brought in for questioning again."

"Why?" I asked.

Ned opened his mouth, when my dad cut in. "Tell her everything," my father told Ned. "Every detail." He looked at me. "We need your big brain on this one," he said.

"Big brain?" I laughed. "A genetic mutation from your side of the family, I believe."

"And a good thing, too. Now put that mass of gray matter to use and figure out what is going on, okay?" My dad gave me a kiss on the top of my head.

"I'll try my best," I told him, then returned my gaze to Ned.

"The police finally found Drake Lonestar. Turns out that unlike you or me, he needs a lot of sleep," Ned said. "He was in bed in his hotel room."

"Performing magic is exhausting," I repeated what Hugo had told me earlier.

"Right." Ned rolled his eyes as if Drake was simply a prima donna who had no idea about real work. "Anyway, the officers discovered that not only was the magician staying in the same hotel as Smallwood, but the two men had rooms across the hall from each other."

I lurched forward in surprise when Ned quickly added, "Apparently the magician was initially put into the same room as Smallwood, but that was a mistake." He shook his head. "When Drake walked in, Smallwood was in the shower. The hotel cleared it up, putting Drake in the room across the hall."

"Shower? That must have been awkward." I chuckled at the thought of walking into a hotel room that was already occupied. "So they had a moment where their paths crossed, but that doesn't prove they knew each other or that Lonestar was involved in the gem theft," I said, furrowing my brow. "Did Lonestar have the missing box or the jewels?"

"No," Ned admitted.

I'd seen Lonestar in handcuffs. "What are the charges against him?"

"He's under investigation for the jewel theft. The police are focusing on the Lonestar and Smallwood connection." Ned added, "That's why Smallwood is being questioned again."

"Under investigation," I echoed Ned's words. "Lonestar shouldn't have been arrested, then. Escorted to court, yes, but no handcuffs."

"I've got this one." I turned to see Officer Fernandez approach. "Lonestar was arrested for disorderly conduct."

I raised my eyebrows. That was unexpected.

"When we showed up, we insisted on knowing how the courthouse disappeared. We figured that if we understood how the trick was done, we could determine how Lonestar managed to break into the evidence locker and steal the box. Instead of answering our questions, Lonestar went crazy and started throwing things around the room."

"He should have known better," I said, wrinkling my brow.

"He doesn't like to be questioned about the magic. We're all clear on that now." She continued, "The police chief believes that Smallwood was working with Lonestar. The theory is that Smallwood stole the gems and put them in the box. He was supposed to give the box to Lonestar. But when Smallwood was arrested and all his belongings were collected by the police, Lonestar panicked. He used his magic to snag the box, and thus, stole the gems for himself." Officer Fernandez's cell phone beeped. "If you'll excuse me, I need to take this." She moved away.

"All this is based on the fact that Drake Lonestar had a room in the hotel across the hall from John Smallwood?" I muttered to myself. The police seemed to be guessing—creating a story about events that they couldn't prove. I knew it. Officer Fernandez knew it. And my dad knew it.

I asked Ned if anyone had found anything suspicious at the hotel.

"No witnesses," he told me. "No box. No gems. Nothing out of place. Even with the disorderly conduct charge, the police are going to have to let Lonestar go soon. They might not let him leave town for a while, but they can't keep here very long."

"This case is getting more and more complicated," I told Ned. "Every time I think we're onto something meaningful, it dissolves into nothing." I bit my lip in frustration.

"I'll find out if Lonestar has said anything relevant to the police," Ned told me.

"My guess is he didn't," I said.

"My guess is you're right," Ned replied.

He left me standing on the courthouse steps, shaking my head and wondering what to do next.

"Nancy, come sit with me." Hugo was resting on a bench just outside the courthouse, staring out toward the empty space where the magic show stage had been the day before. "We can wait to hear what's going on together. It'll be better than waiting alone."

Hugo was so devoted to Drake Lonestar, my admiration for him was growing. Their friendship reminded me of mine with Bess and George. I decided to stay with him until either Ned and my dad came out, Drake was released, or I saw Smallwood.

Bess and George made their way over to us. There was nothing to do but sit there and see if Lonestar would be released.

"Looks like you might not make your train Tuesday," I told Hugo.

"I know." He sighed. "But I'm not canceling the next show until it's absolutely certain that we can't get there in time. The show isn't for a week after we arrive, so we might be able to pull it off. Maybe I'll go ahead without Drake. I can set things up and wait for him there." He glanced at the courthouse. "We'll see."

We sat on that bench waiting for an hour. Then two. At the end of the third hour, Bess was done reorganizing her purse and George had maxed out the data minutes on her smartphone. I'd slept a bit on a nearby patch of grass to make up for the night before, but the truth was we were bored.

Even though it wasn't her job, Officer Fernandez had been bringing us periodic updates and snacks. This time she had bottles of water and granola bars. She was about to leave when Hugo asked, "Want to see some magic?"

Bess brightened. "Sure."

We all gathered around as I shook off the last bit of my sleepiness with a big yawn.

"Can I borrow your handcuffs?" he asked Officer Fernandez. By now we'd spent so much time together that we knew her first name was Faith, that she drove a convertible, and that she lived across the street from her elderly parents.

The officer put a hand on the silver metal cuffs that hung off her police belt. "I don't think it's a good idea. . . ."

"Just for a minute," Hugo said. "I promise they'll be returned to you."

She glanced at the courthouse doors, then to the street. No one was around except for us and a small band of reporters a block away. She pinched her lips together for a short pause before handing Hugo the cuffs.

He passed them to me. "Nancy, check these out. Confirm they are real. I want you to make sure the lock isn't broken and that there aren't any hidden release buttons."

I examined the cuffs and didn't find anything strange.

"Faith," Hugo asked Officer Fernandez, "did I borrow these earlier? Have they been in your possession at all times? Is there any way I might have tampered with them?"

She shook her head. "No to all those questions. I've had them the whole day."

"Put them on me," he told her.

I handed the cuffs back to the officer. She slipped them around Hugo's outstretched hands and locked them tight.

"Where is the key?" Hugo asked, then laughed. "I probably should have asked that before I had you put them on my wrists." He jingled the chain now connecting his wrists together as Officer Fernandez held up a ring of keys.

I had to admit, he was a good showman. I just hoped the trick lived up to his jokes.

"Bess," Hugo asked, "can I use the scarf that's in your purse?"

"Wow!" Bess exclaimed. "How'd you know I had a scarf?"

Hugo rolled his eyes.

"It doesn't take a psychic to know that," I told Bess gently. "We all just watched you clean out your bag."

Bess smiled sheepishly. "Oh, yeah." She reached into her purse and gave Hugo a boldly patterned blue scarf.

"Toss it over my hands," Hugo said, making a scene about how he couldn't possibly do it by himself since he was wearing cuffs.

Bess covered his hands and the handcuffs.

"Do you have a favorite magic word?" Hugo asked me.

"Abracadabra," I answered.

"Right. Now, Nancy, wave your hands over the scarf and say your magic word."

I did as he told me.

"Ta-da!" An instant later Bess's scarf floated to the ground. Hugo picked it up with his free hands. The locks on the cuffs were both open. He gave the handcuffs back to Officer Fernandez and told her to examine them again.

"Well done," she told him. "Remind me not to arrest you."

"How'd you do it?" George asked. I could see the wheels in her brain turning. "Are you double-jointed? Did you put grease on your hands to slip them out? Did you pickpocket the officer's key?"

At that Officer Fernandez checked her key ring. She still had the key.

"It's magic," Hugo said with a chuckle.

"So, you're not just the show's manager and a

security guard . . . you're a magician, too?" I asked.

"Not like Drake." Hugo shrugged. "Drake's art is entirely based on distraction and misdirection."

"Distraction and misdirection," I repeated. "That's magic based on illusion." I was glad that George had taught me about magicians.

Hugo nodded, then went on, "I wanted to be like him at first, but I couldn't figure out how to attract a crowd. I tried doing street shows for a while but never made more than a few bucks and a bus token." He gave Bess her scarf. "All I ever wanted was to be involved in magic. So when the chance came to work for Drake Lonestar, I jumped at it. I tied my dreams to Drake's, and he's done well for us both."

"What about your own dreams?" Bess asked. "After all, that was a really good trick. People would totally pay to see you perform."

"It's too expensive to start: renting venues, travel, advertising, plus the tricks have to get bolder and fancier every year," Hugo said. "I'm happy working for Drake." Hugo stared down at his hands. I could see a faint red line around each wrist where the cuffs had bitten into his skin. I had to admit I had no idea how he'd done it.

Hugo shook out his hands, looked up at the courthouse door, and let loose a long sigh. "I don't know what I'll do if they don't free him soon."

CHAPTER NINE

Careful Considerations

BY DINNERTIME I WAS BACK HOME WITH Ned, John Smallwood, who had been released into my father's custody, and my dad. He couldn't go back to his hotel room anyway, due to all the press gathered in the hallway.

Drake Lonestar was also stuck in River Heights for a few more days. Officer Fernandez had arranged for him to be released to Hugo. The bodyguard was still hopeful they'd be on the Tuesday train out of River Heights, but it didn't look good.

After the day's grueling events—not to mention a sleepless night before—I think we were all ready for a hot meal. Our housekeeper, Hannah Gruen, had just served her famous lasagna when the front door burst open.

"Nancy!" Bess shouted from the front hallway.

"Wait until you see—," George was saying as the two of them rushed up to the table. She stopped short. "Oh . . . is that lasagna?" Whatever she had been about to say was completely lost to the delicious scent of Hannah's dinner.

"Girls?" My father looked from Bess to George and back again.

"Hello, Mr. Drew," Bess said, noticing everyone sitting at the table.

"Sit down, ladies," my father told them, indicating two empty chairs. "Judging by your exciting entry, we are all anxious to see what you've discovered."

Hannah brought them each a plate of lasagna.

Between happy bites, George said to Bess, "Tell them, cuz. You found it."

Bess's mouth was full. She pointed at George and handed her cousin her purse.

George pushed the purse back at Bess.

Before Bess could protest again, I grabbed it. There was a magazine sticking out of the top.

"Are you talking about this?" I asked, checking out the magazine's cover.

"Yes." Bess put down her fork. "The magazine came in yesterday's mail, but with the show and everything, I didn't look until this afternoon."

Bess opened to a page near the middle. I leaned in for a closer look. There was a large photo of Gritty Grand standing with her arms around Ayela and Ariana. All three had the same tilted posture, leaning on their left hips. All three had the same dark hair and dark eyes.

I read the caption: TWINS. We knew that already.

"Keep going," Bess encouraged.

"Daughters!" I leaped up from my chair so fast I nearly knocked Ned's water glass over.

"Whoa," Ned said, grabbing the glass before it spilled. "Why's this news?"

I stepped away from the table and began to pace in the space behind John Smallwood's chair. He was so busy devouring Hannah's lasagna, he didn't look back at me.

"Hang on. . . ." My brain was spinning. "Why *is* this news?" I murmured to myself. It seemed like such a huge revelation. Hugo had lied to us. But how did it connect? "If Gritty Grand's nieces are really her daughters, then . . ." I was mumbling.

"Maybe the jewel heist was a family operation?" Bess asked, forcing me to wonder if I'd spoken my question aloud.

"Yes. I mean, no. I mean . . ." We hadn't had any suspects other than John Smallwood and Drake Lonestar up until this point. Could I add Ayela, Ariana, and their mom to the list?

So Hugo had lied. Was that enough to pursue an investigation of him as well?

"Gritty, Ayela, Ariana," I said to Bess. "Can we connect them to the crime?"

"I've got this one," George chimed in. "The police's number one suspect, Drake Lonestar, is the twins' dad."

"Seriously? Lonestar?" I asked, stunned. "How do you figure that?"

"I did a little Internet digging," George explained, "and apparently it's true. Plus, it makes sense. When their mom was in financial trouble and the girls needed a job, who better to help out than their dad?"

"So is Hugo even dating Gritty?" I asked Bess. She flipped through the magazine until she came to a column called "Hot Couples."

"No," Bess told me. "She's dating Hal Thomas." I looked down at a picture of the designer with her arms around the newest boy-band heartthrob. "She's old enough to be his mom." I grimaced.

"He's the same age as the twins," George agreed.

Bess fluttered her eyelids dramatically. "True love is beyond age."

George punched her in the arm. "You're ridiculous!"

Bess laughed. "You're just jealous. Hoping to snag Hal Thomas for yourself?"

George gagged. "As if! He uses too much hair gel. I'll leave him to Gritty."

"There's one more thing you need to know, Nancy," Bess said, pointing down at the magazine. "The bankruptcy rumors are true. When she talks about her business issues, Gritty actually mentions Drake Lonestar by name."

George went on from there. "She says the exposure from his shows has helped her gain international recognition. Her business isn't solid yet, but things are better."

"Still, she'd like to have more capital. She's hoping to raise a million dollars. She's looking for an investor," Bess said.

"Or a thief," George put in.

"I'm not a thief!" Smallwood roared, leaping up from the table. His small nose twitched, and he was quickly blinking his beady eyes.

I screamed when I saw that he was brandishing a knife.

CHAPTER TEN

The Missing Gems

TURNED OUT JOHN SMALLWOOD WAS HEAD-ing to the counter to cut himself a second serving of lasagna. Everyone laughed at my stunned reaction—even me—but deep inside, I wondered if he might really be the thief. The one who denies the crime most adamantly is often the one who committed it. I wasn't ready to cross Smallwood off the suspect list, nor to defend him like my dad and Ned were. I needed more clues and more evidence.

My adrenaline was pumping as I hustled Bess

and George out of the house. We had a stop to make.

I pulled into the parking lot of the jewelry store just before seven p.m.—a few minutes before closing. George had called ahead to make sure the manager, a woman named Candy Corlean, would be able to stay past closing time if we were late. Candy was tall and so thin and pale that she looked almost ghostly. Her bleached-blond hair was nearly white, and her forehead was taut and wrinkle free.

"Hi there, I'm Nancy Drew." I introduced Bess and George too and launched into an explanation about my dad, the court case, and how we were helping. Candy seemed more than willing to share the details of the night the jewels had disappeared.

The place was dripping with rings, bracelets, necklaces, and even loose stones that had yet to be set. I peeked over my shoulder and saw Bess sigh and smile dreamily. A jewelry store was her happy place. I'm sure she'd have stayed forever if she could.

Candy led us to the counter that had been robbed. The case was empty.

"The police assured me we could reopen for business, but they told me not to touch this particular area," she said, waving her hand over the long glass box that had housed the stolen jewels.

"The missing stones were loose?" I asked.

"Yes," Candy told me. "Stealing a setting would have been far more difficult. We tag all our set jewelry. We don't want to mar the beauty of a stone with a sticky tag, so we leave those unmarked." Moving to a different case, she brought out a tray of rings. Bess leaned in, saying, "Ohhhhhh."

There were small white tags on each ring. "These tags have sensors embedded in them," Candy told us. She pointed up to a row of security cameras that were carefully placed all around the ceiling. "The sensors send information to the security system. If someone tried to walk out without paying, alarms would go off and the police would be here in minutes. The tags are very difficult to remove—the sales reps take them off when they polish each piece for a customer."

"Can I take a closer look?" George asked.

Candy handed her a ring. Bess's fingers twitched as George examined the sensor tag, which also listed the price. She quickly handed the ring back to the shop manager. "Wow, that costs more than a new car. Two cars even."

"It's a—," Candy started to say.

"Flawless sapphire," Bess finished. "Cushion cut and set in platinum."

If Bess had asked for a job just then, it would have been hers. The look on Candy's face told us that she was impressed.

I hadn't actually seen the surveillance tapes from the night the store was robbed. I knew only what Ned had told me: John Smallwood was seen wandering around the shop the night the gems disappeared. He was the last customer to leave that night.

I asked George to pull up a few photos on her smartphone. She quickly found pictures of Drake Lonestar and his daughters from a gossip website.

I zoomed in on the twins and handed the phone

to Candy. "In the days before the robbery, did either of these girls happen to come into the store?"

She took a long look at the photo. "No."

Next I zoomed in on Drake Lonestar's grin. "And him? He's been in town for about a week. Have you seen this man come by?"

"No," Candy replied.

"Are you sure?" I asked lightly, not wanting to imply that I didn't trust her memory.

"With all due respect, Ms. Drew, I have been the eyes and ears of this place for twenty years. The security system is really only in use when I am not here. I have personally stopped nearly ninety shoplifters and prevented six burglaries from taking place," she proudly said. "I am very, very good at my job." She added in a lower voice, "That's why this is extra upsetting. Never has anything like this happened under my watch."

I asked George to bring up another picture—this one of Hugo from Lonestar's website. I turned the phone around so that Candy could see it.

"No," she said firmly. "I've never seen that man."

That left John Smallwood. I pressed my lips together, wondering what I was missing.

"Can I see how the burglar entered the shop?" George asked.

"That's the oddest part," Candy said. "According to the police, none of the doors showed any sign of forced entry. The alarm never went off. Even the security tapes show nothing unusual." She shrugged. "It's as if the stones just disappeared—like magic."

That's what I figured.

Candy went on to tell us that the security equipment was kept in a small room that was always locked; Candy had the only key. While George examined the security system and Bess checked out the cabinet where the gems had been stored, I went outside to make a quick phone call.

Ned answered on the first ring.

"Where are you?" he asked. "Should I run to your side? Do you need to be rescued?" I smiled. It did happen occasionally, though I'd rescued Ned about as many times as he'd rescued me.

"No. Not this time." I laughed. "No knight in shining armor necessary. But you *can* help me out with something. Do you know why John Smallwood was in the jewelry shop that day?"

It had been bothering me for a while. Why would a thief, especially a retired thief, go into a jewelry store? Seems like he was asking for trouble.

"A date," Ned said simply.

I had no idea what he was talking about. "Huh?"

"Apparently, he met Candy at the River Run Coffee Shop the day before. She didn't give him a phone number, but she told him where she worked," Ned explained. "The jewelry store is in the same minimall. So he went to the shop at closing time, then hung out to see if she'd have dinner with him."

"That's kind of romantic," I said.

Ned gave a small laugh. "But while they were out, the store was robbed, and before the night was over, Mr. Smallwood was arrested."

"What a terrible first date," I remarked.

"Hopefully, when your dad clears this up, they can try again," Ned told me.

"Hopefully," I echoed, then thanked him and said good-bye.

Bess was waiting for me. "I just got off the phone with your dad," she said.

"About what?" I asked.

"I wanted to know how many jewels were stolen and their value," she replied.

"I think Ned said the jewels were worth millions," I noted.

"'Millions' is too vague when it comes to gems." Bess snorted. "It's precisely three and a half million dollars in fifteen stones: six emeralds and nine rubies."

"Only fifteen stones?" I was surprised. "Those are some mighty gems."

"Big and flawless. Very valuable." Bess nodded, then said, "I've been thinking about how Gritty wants to raise one million dollars for her clothing line. Three point five is way better than just one measly mil."

"I've been thinking about that too." I took Bess's arm. "Let's get George and move—"

Just then, from the back of the shop, we heard a scream.

"George!" I cried.

CHAPTER ELEVEN

Clue by Clue

"LOOK AT WHAT I FOUND!" GEORGE WAS standing in the security room doorway, gripping a small box.

"The gems?" I asked, expelling a sigh of relief that she was okay.

George snorted. "Better."

"Better than the gems?" Bess said, squinting at her cousin. "What could be better?"

"Videotape!" George cheered.

"Right," Bess said. "I think you *are* sleep deprived."

"No, no," George said. "I mean, yes, I am sleep

deprived, but this is our most important clue yet."

I was listening.

"Nancy, there are some gaping holes in my theory here, but try this," George started. "What if . . ." Her eyes lit up in the darkened room. "What if, after Smallwood left the shop, there was someone else already there? Maybe someone who knew Smallwood, like a partner, or maybe someone else. At this point it doesn't matter."

She shook her head as if to clear it. "Let's just say, once the shop was officially closed, if a person broke into the security room, they'd have had access to the entire system. The security tapes could have been tampered with, and whoever stole the jewels could have simply played footage from any other night." She held up the tape box. "The tapes would have shown that all was quiet even though the thief was inside. Then there is just the matter of disabling the alarm and opening the gem case."

"Sounds possible," I said. "I like that idea better than to think the gems magically disappeared."

"Me too," George said adamantly. "There's always an explanation for everything." She handed me the tape. "The police missed this one. There's a backup unit for the security equipment in a cabinet. That machine had been tampered with; it was set to play, not record."

Candy let us use the machine, and we quickly discovered that George was right. The tape showed looped footage of a quiet night. She'd found our most important clue so far. Someone had been in the security room when Candy left for her date.

"I'm not sure how they got in," George was saying as we walked from the room. "I mean, this door was locked, the front door was locked, the back—"

"Ewww!" Bess hopped from foot to foot, making gagging sounds. "I stepped in gum! Gross."

"Gum?" Candy asked. "There's no food allowed in this shop. That's why I go to the coffee shop at ten, noon, and three for all my scheduled breaks. No food. No drinks. And certainly no gum." She handed Bess a tissue. "Someone will be fired!"

"It's a huge wad!" Bess said, peeling it off her shoe. "Blech."

"It's not just gum." George took the tissue and peered inside. "I mean, it is, but I think it's also part of the crime." She paused, staring at the gum. "Maybe the thief planted it here on purpose. Though I don't think this gum was used in the heist. I checked the doors and there was no sign of anything gummy in the locks."

Candy looked crushed. "After all these years, someone slipped by me." She put her hands on her hips. "I'll call the police. They should check the locks again and reinterview my employees."

"This is a highly professional job," I told her. "The gum, the videotape, the gems—your employees probably aren't suspects."

As we left, Candy was on the phone arranging for a new security company to come install an upgraded system.

"Good sleuthing!" I congratulated my friends. "We are definitely getting somewhere!"

"Right," Bess said with a sigh. "All we have left to

do is to figure out is who did it, why, and where they put the jewels."

"No problem," I said with a laugh. "I'm hoping we'll find out more at our next stop."

It was a little after ten p.m. when I pulled into the Riverview parking lot. At night the place looked even more shabby and run-down than it had in the daylight. I hoped the twins were awake. We needed to talk to them.

"You'd think if the girls stole the gems they'd have at least kept some of the money for a hotel upgrade," Bess said, wrinkling her nose.

"I don't think the gems have been sold yet," George said. "Whoever took them needs to get far away from here first."

"But even if the twins *do* have the gems, they might be stuck in this motel anyway. Hugo told me that these performances are expensive to run." I held the door for my friends. "I guess that's why the staff stays at the cheap places while the magician goes to stay at the fancy resort."

"Even if he was escaping from a crazy stalker-fan, the twins might resent their dad for leaving them here," George said. "I know I would."

"If they *are* angry, no one's said anything." I recalled all the conversations I'd had with Ayela and Ariana. They'd never even let on that Lonestar was their dad—certainly not that he'd moved on to better digs and stuck them with Hugo.

The hotel lobby was quiet. The only sign of life was a desk clerk at the counter. The young woman looked bored, like she wished she was anywhere else. Her long brown hair hung over one charcoaled eye.

When we approached the desk, she looked up and pinned that one eye on me. "Can I help you?"

Bess moved in and flashed a smile. "We're looking for Drake Lonestar's two assistants. Could you tell us what room they're in?"

The woman picked up a pen and twirled it. "I'm not supposed to give out information on our guests."

It might have been the first time in Bess's life that her oozing charm didn't work.

George gave her a small, sympathetic smile.

Undeterred, Bess tried again. "But we know Ayela and Ariana. We were supposed to meet them"—she stopped to check her watch—"*twenty* minutes ago." Bess threw George a dirty look over her shoulder, as if it was George's fault we had only arrived now.

"Please," Bess said in the sweetest voice I'd ever heard.

"Oh, um . . ." The clerk paused and twirled her pen some more. "Whatever." She scribbled the number on a slip of paper. "Go ahead. Let them fire me. I hate this job."

As we walked away, Bess grinned at George and said, "The Marvin charm hasn't failed me yet."

George rolled her eyes.

After a quick elevator ride, we were standing in front of room 406. The TV was on inside. I knocked on the hotel room door.

Ayela opened it. "Hey!" She was super cheery as she let us inside. "Welcome!"

The room was tiny. Two beds and a roll-away sleeper were stuffed wall to wall. In fact, so much furniture had been crammed into the small space that there was nowhere to stand. I peeked into the tiny bathroom; the fact that an architect had managed to fit a shower, toilet, and sink in there might have been the most impressive magic trick of the past week.

Deep-red wallpaper, stained with age and peeling from decay, made the room so dark I had to squint to see Ariana sitting on the bed, next to her dad.

Drake Lonestar.

"I was wondering when you'd show up," he said.

I didn't mean to be rude by not replying, but my tongue was tied. Above Drake's head, above where the roll-away sleeper was squashed up against the wall, there were holes. Lots and lots of little holes.

"Darts!" I practically shouted the word, scanning the floor. "Aha!" I found one halfway behind the nightstand. I grabbed it and held it up like a trophy. This was a big clue.

George pointed at Lonestar. "So you were already

in River Heights when you decided to come to River Heights!"

"George, are you saying that the video of Lonestar throwing darts at a map is fake?" Bess asked.

"The video was planned and carefully edited," George said, not moving her eyes from Lonestar's face. "I should have realized! From what I've read, videos are often used in illusion magic because they are so easy to manipulate. That means that if they're done right, they seem live. Drake knew he was coming to River Heights."

"Don't look at me with those disappointed eyes. Your courthouse was perfect for what I wanted to do," Lonestar told George.

"But it was a bold lie," George accused. "You made a video about how you 'chose' River Heights with a single dart throw." She glanced at the pockmarked wall. "Apparently, it took more than one toss."

Lonestar laughed. "Hugo is a terrific filmmaker. The darts took a lot of practice for me, but the video was done in a single recording. "

He asked me to grab a deck of cards from the nightstand. "Once I could pin the map, I moved on to other tricks. Check this one out." He took the cards, shuffled them, and fanned them in front of me. "Pick a card. Don't show me which one." Drake rose from the bed and handed me a pen. "Write your name on it."

I took the ace of spades and wrote *NANCY* in bold letters across the top.

He opened the deck to a random spot. "Put in the card." I did, and he shuffled the deck. Then he told me to shuffle. I ran the cards through my fingers several times and handed the deck back to him.

"I'm going to throw a dart at the wall three times," Drake told me, taking the dart I'd picked up off the floor. "Two for practice, and on the third, I'll toss up the deck." The first shot landed in the wall, knocking down bits of dry plaster as it stuck. He took back the dart and did the same thing.

With the third throw, Drake Lonestar tossed up the deck of cards. They fluttered through the air as the dart soared from his fingertips to the wall.

"Take a look," he told me.

The dart was stuck in the wall. There was a single playing card pinned there, speared through the point. I peeled it off the wall. "It's mine," I said, showing Bess and George the ace of spades with my name written on it.

"Nicely done," George told Drake.

He said, "We wanted to come to River Heights, but we had to make it look coincidental. Besides"—he removed the dart and put away the cards—"magic is always a kind of lying. Like those flowers I made appear out of thin air; you know they didn't just come from nothing. I say the courthouse 'disappeared,' but you know it really didn't." He paused and turned to face me. "Have you figured out how I did that one yet, Nancy?"

"No." I shook my head. "I've been trying to take your advice and not overthink the magic."

"Perfect!" He sat down and leaned back against a pillow. "That means you accepted the lie."

"I suppose I did." I glanced at Bess and George. "On some level, we all did."

"Good," Lonestar said. "If people didn't completely suspend their logical reasoning, I wouldn't have a job."

I nodded. He was right. I supposed it didn't make a difference how he'd decided to come to our town, except for one thing: Everyone already knew that Drake Lonestar was around the night the gems were stolen from the jewelry shop, but now it wasn't a coincidence that he'd been in River Heights. He had actually *planned* to be here. That made it even more suspicious. He'd had plenty of time to plan a show as well as a heist.

As hard as I was trying to put other suspects on my list, Drake kept making it impossible. Every clue kept coming back to him. Even Hugo couldn't protect Drake from the evidence mounting against him.

"Where's Hugo?" I asked Lonestar. My dad said that Lonestar had been released into Hugo's custody. Shouldn't the bodyguard have been around?

"He went to the resort," Drake said. "I left all my gear in my room, but I can't go back, not even to help him. The press is camped out there."

I nodded. Smallwood was at my house for the same reason.

He waved his hand at the roll-away and groaned. "I'm bunking with the girls until this legal mess is resolved."

"Why didn't the media follow you here?" I asked him.

Lonestar grinned. "Hugo spread a rumor that I was planning to go to the resort later tonight."

"Another lie?" I couldn't help myself; it just burst out.

"I suppose," Drake Lonestar said. "This time, a small white one for protection. It's the same reason Hugo lied about Ayela and Ariana being Gritty Grand's nieces instead of her daughters. And why he's been telling the press that he's dating Gritty."

He went on, "I work hard to distance myself from anyone who might use my family to get close to me. Hired employees, even if they are related to a top designer, are definitely less interesting than a magician's daughters. The idea of Hugo and Gritty dating is less scandalous than her being my ex. All of these are red herrings meant to throw the paparazzi off my trail."

"The Internet is a mix of truth and lies," George said. "If someone really wanted to find out about you, it wouldn't be so hard."

"We throw a lot of misinformation out there to cover the facts. If a fan or the press wants to know details, we have to at least make them work for them. That's what Hugo says, and I trust him completely. He's a great bodyguard and manager."

While George and I had been talking to Lonestar, the twins had been giving Bess a preview of Gritty's new collection—previously unseen pieces that would appear in upcoming fashion shows. I knew that Bess was probably thrilled to see the clothing, but she was also deciding whether the twins might be our thieves.

That had been the real goal of this visit. Discovering the darts had been a bonus.

When she joined George and me, she shook her head. I got the message: She wasn't sure.

Bess whispered to us. "I tried to get them to talk about accessories, like jewelry, but they aren't interested. They wanted to talk about leggings and tunics and the staples of a wardrobe." She shrugged. "Even when I tried to bring up their mom's money issues, they wouldn't go there." Bess lowered her voice even further and said, "I frankly don't think either of them are sharp enough to pull off this kind of crime." She quickly added, "The only suspicious thing I noticed was that they both like chewing gum."

That was something. I wondered if it was the same kind of gum Bess had stepped in at the jewelry store.

"But what about the magic?" George asked. "They know how Drake does his illusions. So much of this theft seems similar to magic tricks. Do you think they can do any tricks of their own?"

"Well," Bess replied, "Ariana can remove her socks without taking off her shoes."

I laughed a bit too loudly.

"What's so funny?" Drake asked.

"Nothing," I hedged. "It's late. We need to go."

After we said our good-byes, I made a plan for the next hour. I'd drop off Bess and George, and then jot down some notes on what we'd discovered. We'd made good progress, but I wasn't sure what it all meant. I needed to think. I also needed to sleep.

Bess opened the door to Lonestar's hotel room. We were stunned to find the hallway crowded with police and journalists.

Officer Fernandez pushed past me. She announced, "Mr. Lonestar, you need to come with me. We found the missing box in your hotel room."

CHAPTER TWELVE

~

Inside the Box

WITH THIS DEVELOPMENT, I WAS CERTAIN we'd be up all night again, but luckily, Bess, George, and I were able to catch a few hours of sleep before heading to the courthouse. When I spoke to Ned shortly after the police showed up, he assured me there was no reason to hurry. The paperwork would take a while, and then the lawyers had to get there. That would take time too.

When I did arrive at the courthouse, well rested, I realized that I had forgotten to charge my phone. I turned down the screen's brightness and muted the sound and did everything else I could think of to save power. I was waiting for a call from Ned or my dad—one I couldn't risk missing.

Because the box surfacing impacted John Smallwood, my dad and Ned were inside the courthouse waiting to be briefed. Until every shadow about Smallwood and Lonestar was brought to light, Dad's client wouldn't be let off the hook.

Lonestar had refused an attorney the day before, but this was more serious. Now he had brought in his own lawyer. And it was none other than River Heights' own Madeline Summers.

Madeline was a tough nut who had worked with my dad on many cases. Though I wasn't sure how Lonestar had found her, I had no doubt she'd give her all to Drake. The one thing about Madeline was that she worked alone. That meant she didn't want to hear from any outside detectives—namely me. In the past, she'd made it crystal clear that I was to stay away from her clients. I was certain this would be no different. But just because Madeline Summers didn't want me around didn't mean I would back down from my personal investigation.

My phone rang.

"Ned?" I shouted as I stabbed the talk button. "What's going on?"

"The police found the missing box in Lonestar's hotel room at the Towering Heights Resort," he said.

"Oh." I'd assumed that was what happened. "And the gems?"

"The box is still sealed. The locksmith is on his way."

My shoulders dropped. This was the most exciting part of the investigation, and Madeline Summers would surely try to keep me out of the judge's chambers. I'd be lucky if my dad and Ned were allowed in, since they weren't Lonestar's attorneys.

"The locksmith needs an escort into the building," Ned told me. "Three escorts, actually. There are passes at the security desk for you, Bess, and George."

I was shocked. "I can't believe Mrs. Summers would agree to let me anywhere near her client. How'd you do it?"

"Do you believe in magic?" Ned asked. His voice had a light chuckle to it.

"That's the question of the moment, isn't it?" Even though he couldn't see me through the phone, I smiled.

"Come straight to the judge's chambers," Ned said, then hung up.

The locksmith's van was already pulling into the parking lot. We ran to meet the elderly man. He was wearing a suit that was frayed with age, but he had close-cut hair and a clean-shaven face. The sign on his truck read GALLOWAY GETS IT DONE.

"You'll need a 505 wrench with a needle-nose tip for this one," George told Mr. Galloway before we'd actually introduced ourselves.

"Really?" he looked at her with a shocked expression. "You've seen this mystery box?"

"No," George admitted. "I'm just saying that's what I'd take if I were you."

"All righty then." He just shook his head as he grabbed that wrench plus a few others.

"We're here to show you the way," I said.

"Lead on," Mr. Galloway replied.

Judge Nguyen's chamber was packed. In one corner there was the magician and his lawyer. In the other were my dad and Ned. Ned tipped his head to me when I entered with George, Mr. Galloway, and Bess.

Judge Nguyen sat in her oversize leather chair, gazing at us all, with the mystery box on her desk.

The box was made of the most beautiful polished wood I'd ever seen: red mahogany with thin ribbons of a lighter blond oak. Engraved into the sides and top were ornate swirls and designs that looked as if they came from India, with interlocking loops and flares. The depth of the carvings made the wood shine and shimmer, giving the effect that the wood itself was flowing like a river.

I couldn't take my eyes off those carvings. The mysterious box held me in a spell.

Judge Nguyen stood and said, "This box was originally found among John Smallwood's things at the

Towering Heights Resort. He has sworn all along that the box does not belong to him and that he does not know how it came to be in his room."

She looked at my dad and continued, "Because Mr. Drew and Ned Nickerson are Smallwood's legal team, I feel that it is important for them to be here at the opening. If jewels are inside, Mr. Smallwood will be immediately arrested, pending a full investigation." She looked at a notepad on the side of her desk. "I presume he is standing by at your house, Mr. Drew?"

My dad nodded.

I threw my dad a smile. Smallwood and Hannah were probably sitting at the table, enjoying leftover lasagna.

The judge glanced at the locksmith, who was clearly ready to get to work. She reviewed pertinent facts. "The box was collected at the hotel and moved to an evidence locker in the courthouse for safekeeping until it could be opened. Sometime during Mr. Lonestar's magic act on Saturday, the box disappeared from the evidence locker. It has been missing until today."

"Just because it reappeared in my client's hotel room does not mean that the box or its contents belong to Mr. Lonestar," Madeline Summers put in.

"True," the judge said. She turned to me. "Nancy Drew, you were at the magic show the day the box disappeared. I've been told that you and your friends have some information to share."

I glanced at Ned. So that was how he gotten us in; he'd promised that I'd reveal what we'd discovered.

I bit my tongue. I wasn't ready for this. I hadn't solved the mystery yet. But if I declined to comment, I'd be kicked out of the room and miss the box opening.

I sighed. "Everything we've discovered points to Drake Lonestar as the gem thief," I said.

"Objection!" Mrs. Summers stomped to the center of the room. "Miss Drew cannot make accusatory statements like that! She has no proof that my client is the thief."

I directed my gaze at the judge and said, "I'm not saying he did it, Your Honor. I'm saying that everything is *pointing* to the likelihood that he took the gems."

"Go on, Miss Drew," the judge told me.

"Drake Lonestar was in town several days before the burglary. He knew his courthouse trick would be performed here in River Heights. His personal time-line fits the timeline of the crime, and his arrival wasn't a coincidence, like he'd led us all to believe." I looked back over my shoulder at Lonestar, who radiated a cool calmness.

"The lies keep piling up from there. His bodyguard, Hugo, told everyone that he was dating Lonestar's ex-wife, Gritty Grand. Hugo has no such relationship with Ms. Grand. Lonestar came to town with his daughters, claiming they were Gritty's nieces.

"Although there's no proof he has ever met John Smallwood, Lonestar moved from the Riverview Hotel to the Towering Heights Resort and was placed in the room across the hall from the suspected thief." I had one last thing to say. "The break-in at the jewelry shop showed some classic hallmarks of a magic act."

I explained about the video loop and the gum on the floor. "Magic is about illusion. Often elements are set up in advance of the actual trick." I looked directly at Drake. "Right, Mr. Lonestar?"

"Enough!" Madeline Summers roared. She turned to her client. "Don't answer that."

Drake Lonestar settled his eyes on mine. I felt a chill go up my spine as he glared at me.

Judge Nguyen cleared her throat, demanding the attention of everyone in the room. "It does seem, for now, that the evidence points to the magician as the gem thief." She told Officer Collins, who'd been standing near the door, "Take the handcuffs off Mr. Lonestar. He's not going anywhere." Then she pointed at her desk. "Let's open this box and see where this case goes next."

CHAPTER THIRTEEN

Unlocking the Magic

I WANTED TO STAND NEXT TO MR. GALLOWAY, the locksmith, but the judge asked us all to keep back. Mr. Galloway turned the box over on the desk and raised a pair of pliers. Frowning, he rotated the box to one side, then the other.

"There's no latch," he said, with a confused, blank expression. "No seams or obvious entry point."

Mr. Galloway raised the box and looked like he was about to shake it.

"No!" Bess shrieked.

"What is your objection?" the judge asked Bess.

"Oh, please tell me the police never shook that box," Bess muttered as she stepped up beside the locksmith.

"I don't know whether they did," the judge replied. "Why?"

Bess explained, "The gems that are missing are very delicate rubies and emeralds. If they are inside and knocked together, it's likely they might get scratched. Or worse"—her eyes went wide with horror—"they might chip! The value of those stones is based on their condition."

Judge Nguyen nodded and told the locksmith, "Be more careful."

"Yes, ma'am," he agreed. He continued to search for an opening to the box.

We all watched closely as time ticked away. Madeline Summers was getting impatient. By the way she was tapping her toe, I could tell she was ready to grab a hammer and open the box herself.

The carvings on the box continued to mesmerize me, especially as the locksmith rotated it and sunlight began to stream in through the room's window. The brightness of the light striking the wood was hypnotizing.

That's when I saw it.

At an intersection where the two colors of wood met, there was a hole. It was smaller than the dart marks in Drake's hotel room and too tiny for any of the locksmith's tools, as far as I could tell.

I nudged Bess. "Can I borrow an earring?" I whispered.

She looked at me as if I was crazy. "This isn't really the time to play dress up," she hissed.

"Please?" I held out my hand. She gave me a small pearl on a gold post. "Keep the back," I said, pinching the pearl in my fingers.

"Uh, can I have a try?" I asked Mr. Galloway.

"If it's okay with the judge," he said with a shrug. "I've never seen a box like this. Staring at it makes my head feel foggy."

"Mine too," I told him. "But it also gave me some clarity."

"That's because it's a meditation mandala," Drake said.

"Stop right there," his lawyer put up a hand. "Not another word."

"I think it's in the interest of the court if he speaks. Go on, Mr. Lonestar," the judge prodded.

"The outside carving is for meditation. The ornate design is called a mandala. This particular design is meant to open one's heart and allow for profound insight."

"Are you certain this box does not belong to you?" the judge said. "You seem to know a lot about it."

"The box is not mine," Drake said in a calm voice.

"I see," the judge said. "Then you do not know how to open it?"

Drake shook his head. "No. Each box is uniquely created for the person who purchased it."

Madeline Summers glared at him. Drake shut his mouth.

"May I try?" I asked.

"You seem quite certain, Miss Drew," Judge Nguyen said. "Have *you* seen this box before?"

"No." I said. "But after staring at the box for so long, I felt an odd spark of insight, and then I saw the keyhole."

"Go ahead," the judge told me.

"Can you open the curtain a bit more?" I asked Bess. The sunlight had moved, and I wanted it to fully illuminate the carvings. I had lost the keyhole for a moment, but as the sun hit the box anew, that tiny hole became so prominent that I couldn't believe no one had seen it before.

I took the end of Bess's earring and slowly pushed it into the pinhole. The box top opened along seam lines that had been previously invisible.

I felt a heated rush as everybody in the room crowded around me. All eyes peered past my shoulders into the empty space within that ornate box.

"Nothing," Ned said with a sigh. "All this for nothing."

"There's a false bottom," Bess said.

"How do you know?" I asked her.

"There's always a false bottom," she replied, grinning at me. "Don't you pay attention to your own mysteries, Nancy?"

I laughed. It was true; whenever we came to a dead end, it was never *really* the end.

I searched the interior, which was made out of the same wood as the outside, beautifully polished but not carved. I tipped the box toward the sunlight.

"I don't see—," I began, when George reached over my shoulder. She tucked her finger into a groove I hadn't noticed and lifted out a large piece of the wooden interior. Beneath that was, indeed, a hidden compartment.

I gasped. Inside were three glittering red rubies.

CHAPTER FOURTEEN

Flawless

THEY WERE BEAUTIFUL. THE PUREST RED I'd ever seen. I had no doubt they were real. Bess reached in to touch one, but the judge stopped her.

"Wait. We need a forensic specialist to take a look at that."

The judge told Officer Fernandez, "Officer, please bring Mr. Smallwood to the courthouse. We need to clear this up. The box was originally in John Smallwood's room, then it disappeared, only to reappear in Drake Lonestar's room. The resolution to this crime is somewhere between these two men."

"On my way." Officer Fernandez rushed from the room.

"Everyone else, stay put," the judge commanded.

Bess pulled me away from the others. "Those stones are probably worth just enough to cover Gritty Grand's debts. This doesn't look good for Lonestar."

George joined us. "But what about the other gems? There is another two and a half million dollars' worth of emeralds and rubies still missing."

Bess glanced over her shoulder at Drake, who was conferring with Madeline Summers. "I don't think there's any way to avoid him going to jail. Even if they never find the other stones, so much of what we've discovered points to Drake as the thief."

"I think that's the point," I said. "It seems like a setup to me. With Drake Lonestar in jail, no one will question where the other gems are. They'll assume Drake took them, hid them, destroyed them, whatever." I sighed. "Someone is planning to get away with the other stones . . . and knows it's likely that part of the mystery will remain unsolved."

"Unless you solve it," George said, putting her hand on my shoulder.

My head was spinning. No matter how many times I reviewed the evidence, it all came back to Drake. What was I missing?

There was one thing gnawing at me. . . . I hadn't had time to look up Harry Houdini's famous jail escape trick that George had mentioned at her house the previous day, and I wanted to know more. I asked George to tell me about it.

"It was 1904," she said. "Houdini was already known for his handcuff escapes but had added jail escapes to his show when he was on tour. Once, at Scotland Yard, the chief constable asked him to do a trick on the spot, without any preparation. They locked him in a cell and triple-locked the door. Then they locked the iron gate leading to the cell block. Five minutes later, he arrived in a public hallway!"

"Amazing," Bess said.

"Yes," I agreed. "Are there theories of how he did it?"

"No one knows for sure," George told me. "But

some say he might have visited the cell block earlier. Apparently, he had a kind of a wax that he could put in the locks, make a mold, then create a key to use later. The rumor is that he had a false sole on his shoe and hid the keys there."

"But no one knows for sure?" I asked.

"There are guesses as to how he got the keys he needed, but they always come back to the fact that he had them," George said.

"Thanks." I was considering George's story when I heard a rattling sound and looked up to see Drake Lonestar staring directly at me, dangling a pair of handcuffs.

Madeleine Summers had a look of horror on her face. "What are you doing?" she hissed at him.

"Mr. Lonestar," Judge Nguyen said sharply. "May I ask why you have a pair of handcuffs in your possession?"

"A magician never leaves home without them," he replied with a chuckle. He again fixed me with his intense stare.

And just like that, I was certain that Drake Lonestar was not the jewel thief.

"We gotta go," I told Bess and George. "Hurry!"

I gave the judge some lame excuse about parking in a tow-away zone and headed for the door.

Suddenly the judge's chamber door burst open.

"I came as soon as I heard!" A woman quickly crossed the room and gave Drake Lonestar a huge hug. "Oh, darling! How can I help you?"

Bess put a hand to her mouth and choked out, "That's Gritty Grand!"

CHAPTER FIFTEEN

Lies Liars Tell

"WILL A LIAR LIE ABOUT HIS OWN LIE?"
Bess asked as we piled into my car.

"And if this liar is lying, which lie is he lying about?"
George asked, raising an eyebrow.

"The liar who lied is not the lying liar," I said, feeling satisfied that I'd finally solved the case.

It took a few phone calls to figure out where I needed to go. The twins were alone at the Riverview, and I knew who was at the courthouse. That left one person . . . and one place for that person to be, but time was running out.

After a short drive, we pulled up to the Towering Heights Resort. I let the valet take my car. The guy's eyes brightened when he saw Bess.

"Oh, good grief," George complained. "I think the magician here is Bess. She's got all of River Heights under some spell."

"It's not a spell," Bess countered. "It's my natural charm."

"What can I do for you ladies?" the valet asked as he helped Bess out of the backseat. His long hair was combed back, showing his deep-blue eyes. I had to admit, he was pretty cute.

"Can you watch the car? We have to run." I grabbed Bess's arm. We'd be standing there all day if I didn't take charge.

"See you later," the valet said.

"Okay," Bess replied, looking back at him over her shoulder.

"Yuck," George gagged. "He wasn't asking you on a date, you know."

"How do you know? Maybe he was," Bess said.

It wasn't hard to find Lonestar's hotel room. The gaggle of reporters on the thirteenth floor gave away the exact spot. I couldn't believe that the Towering Heights even had a thirteenth floor. I knew from years of detective work that most hotels don't have them. Through the crowd I could see that yellow plastic police tape blocked off both Lonestar's room and the one across the hall where Smallwood had been staying.

"Thirteen is the bad-luck floor," Bess said. "Of course they are both being accused of theft. If they had stayed on twelve or fourteen, none of this would have happened."

George stared at Bess as if she was nuts. "What are you talking about?"

Bess shrugged. "Just saying."

"Ridiculous," George countered. "Superstition is contrary to science."

"And being a Virgo rising in the house of Aries, you'd say exactly that," Bess replied.

To calm things down, I stepped between Bess and George, just like someone whose intellect is ruled by Sagittarius would; at least that's what Bess told me.

We made our way down the hall and immediately discovered why Lonestar and Smallwood had stayed away from the resort.

Microphones and cameras were thrust in our faces.

"Nancy!"

"Nancy Drew!"

Several people were calling my name at once. There must have been twenty reporters plus their film crews gathered.

"Is Drake Lonestar the gem thief?" a woman shouted at me.

"I was told by my sources that it's that woman from the jewelry store! I hear you went there to accuse her."

"The nieces!" someone said, but a man corrected her, "You mean the daughters."

"Ariana," someone furnished a name.

"Ayela," another called out.

"That other guy!"

I wasn't sure exactly who the reporter was talking

about, so I asked. "Hugo?" I wrinkled my brow.

"No! John Smallwood! He was caught on tape!"

The voices and accusations swirled around me. It seemed that the city was suddenly filled with a lot of amateur detectives, all with different suspects to accuse.

"I hear it's Gritty Grand! Rumor is that she and that boyfriend singer of hers are in town in disguise."

Wow. They'd found that out fast. Gritty was for sure in town. But the boyfriend? From the way she'd greeted Drake Lonestar, I wasn't convinced she had a boyfriend.

"Where's Lonestar now?" When a reporter asked me that, I knew my hunch had been correct. These reporters didn't know that Drake had been arrested. Otherwise they'd have left the hotel and headed to the courthouse. They were still hoping he'd show up here.

"Nancy! Who stole the jewels? Do you know?" a man at the back of the pack yelled to me.

I'd had enough. Even if I had known, I wasn't going to tell the tall guy from Channel Four before I told the judge, the police, my dad, or Ned. "Let's go," I told my friends.

Knocking on the hotel suite door would have started a huge media frenzy, ruining my subtle approach, so we turned around and headed back toward the elevators. The reporters continued to shout out at me, but luckily, no one followed. They weren't leaving the hallway, just in case someone more interesting than me happened by.

We went back outside to the valet.

"Hey! We can go get a coffee now if you want. It's almost time for my break." In a blink he moved from behind the valet stand to Bess's side.

She smiled at George with an *I told you so* grin.

I checked his name tag. "Look, Sawyer, we have a problem. I need to get to the thirteenth floor, past the reporters, and into Drake Lonestar's hotel room. Can you help?"

I knew it was a lot to ask, but I was desperate. There was something in that room that would solve this case once and for all. I was sure of it.

"Hmm," Sawyer said. "The thirteenth, you say?"

"Yes." I explained the reporter problem.

He pursed his lips and said, "Look, I know who you are, Nancy Drew. You're famous."

I blushed. "Not really."

"I was at the magic show. Drake Lonestar is fantastic. I've always loved magic. In fact, I'm a card-carrying member of the River Heights Magic Club."

I didn't even know there was a River Heights Magic Club. "We are going to prove he didn't steal the gems," I said.

Bess flashed a toothy grin. "And we'd appreciate your help," she added.

"I'll do it for Drake," he said, winking at Bess.

Exactly three minutes later we were getting off the staff elevator on the thirteenth floor.

"I could have gotten a key," Sawyer said, "but as far as I can tell, there's no way around the reporters."

"We need to bypass them," I confirmed.

"We could have pulled the fire alarm," George suggested. "Chased them out and cleared the hall."

"Or climbed in over the balcony," Bess said.

"Nah, this is safer," Sawyer told us. He opened a door marked EMPLOYEES ONLY. "My dad works on the maintenance crew at this hotel. I've been hanging out here since I was a kid. I know every nook and cranny by heart. When I got old enough, they let me bus tables in the café; now I park cars. I'll do maintenance with my dad this summer." He grinned. "I'm working my way up."

"Couldn't you get in trouble for this?" George asked, following Bess up a ladder in the maintenance closet. "I'd hate for us to get you fired."

"Ah, it's okay. It's an adventure," he chuckled. "I like adventures." Sawyer scooted into the crawl space below a heat duct. We climbed in behind him. He was in the lead, with Bess and George in the middle, while I brought up the rear. "When I was a kid," he continued, "I used to come up here all the time. The owners of this hotel used the highest-rated titanium alloys in construction. Not only are the vents—"

"—strong and light, but they are also incredibly

heat resistant," George finished. There was just enough room to crawl on our knees, but not enough to move comfortably around.

Unable to turn his body, Sawyer looked back, past Bess, to George. He'd brought a flashlight and shone it in her face. "What are you, an astrophysicist?"

George laughed. "Maybe someday."

"Well, I'm studying to be one," Sawyer said. "The university here has a great program for students who hope to become astronauts. I can't imagine a greater adventure than visiting the stars!" He twisted around and continued to lead us down the vents. When the vents split in two directions, we went left.

Our leader stopped so suddenly, Bess ran into him, which meant George bumped Bess and I ran into George. We were a tangled mess of arms and legs.

"Shhh," Sawyer said. "We're here." He spun his flashlight around and this time pointed it at me. "Where do you want to go in? We could drop into the bedroom or the living room."

"Is there an opening in the bathroom?" That

seemed like a safe place. We didn't have a ladder on this end, so it might be easier to step down to the sink or tub instead of risking broken bones by jumping out onto the cold floor.

"One bathroom, coming right up," Sawyer said as he moved slightly to the right and removed a panel from the vent. He reached out and took a tile from the ceiling before lowering himself out of the vent.

I heard him land, then say, "Okay, Bess—"

"What on earth?!" A man's deep voice, low and threatening, came from below. I heard Sawyer squeal.

"Who are you? What are you doing here?" The man's voice rattled the vents.

Smashed up behind Bess and George, and now without the flashlight, I couldn't see anything. But I knew that voice.

We'd found our jewel thief.

CHAPTER SIXTEEN

All the Answers

SAWYER'S NECK WAS FIRMLY IN HUGO'S grasp.

"Let him go!" I cried from the ceiling. When I'd realized what was happening below, I'd thrown myself over Bess and George, flattening them so I could slither like a snake to the front.

From where I was, I could see that Sawyer was turning blue.

"Please, Hugo." I wasn't sure he could even hear me. As a bodyguard, he was trained to act first, think later.

"Hugo!" I raised my voice. "I'm coming down."

There was no way to turn my body around, so Bess and George each took one of my legs and lowered me to the sink counter. I grabbed the towel bar to slow my decent, but ended up ripping it off the wall as I tumbled into a heap at Hugo's feet, knocking over the trash can; little bits of wood and used sugar packets tumbled out and littered the floor.

Hugo let go of Sawyer, turning toward me with a surprised expression.

Sawyer coughed and sputtered as the color came back into his face.

"Are you all right?" Bess shouted from the vent.

"He better not have damaged your ability to solve complex mathematic equations!" George yelled. "An astronaut needs math!"

"What's two plus two?" I asked Sawyer.

"Four," he choked out.

"He's fine," I called to Bess and George. "Come on down."

"Nancy Drew?" Hugo stepped back as if seeing me for the first time. "I thought I'd caught a thief."

"We need to talk." I walked out of the bathroom, hoping Hugo would follow. I wanted to give Sawyer space to help my friends out of the vents, and I hoped that by leaving the room, I could keep everyone safe until the police arrived. We were so in tune with one another that I knew either George or Bess would call the police.

Pretending my heart wasn't beating wildly, I sat on the couch. I'd have preferred not to confront Hugo like this, but it was too late to back out. It all came down to this moment.

"What are you doing here?" Hugo asked me.

"I came to find you," I said. "Drake Lonestar has been arrested for the crime you committed. You stole the jewels."

"What are you talking about?" Hugo's face was expressionless.

"Don't pretend you don't know," I said to him. "You're the one who left the mystery box filled with one million dollars' worth of gems in Drake's room and then called the police. After that, you called the press."

I waved my hand toward the door to the hallway. In the quiet lull I could hear the reporters chatting with one another.

"The reporters came here and piled up in the hallway. They don't know about the arrest yet, and you've made sure the timing works on your schedule. You're using them as part of this massive illusion you've created."

Hugo didn't deny it. He wasn't confirming it either.

"I realized this was the best place for you to hide out. If you'd been at the Riverview, Ayela and Ariana would have insisted you go with them to the courthouse. You weren't about to rush to *support* your friend, whom you'd just betrayed, so this was the most convenient spot to wait. As soon as the reporters hear the news, they'll immediately rush to the courthouse. Then you can quietly leave, completely unnoticed."

"You're talking nonsense, Nancy," he said.

"I don't think so. I'm confident I have this all figured out. In fact, you told me you'd committed this crime yourself," I said to Hugo. "Not in those exact words, but close enough. It just took me a while to understand."

"I'd never say that." Hugo sat across from me, which made me wary. He met my gaze and said, "Drake Lonestar stole the gems."

"That's what you wanted us all to believe," I said. "You told me yourself that magic was all about distraction and misdirection."

He nodded. "That I did. It is. So?"

"I've been thinking about that ever since. Everything in this case pointed to Drake Lonestar. You set up Lonestar to *appear* to be the thief while you took the gems."

"It's not wise to accuse someone without proof," Hugo said, starting to rise. "Tell me, Miss Drew. What is it that you *think* you know?"

I glanced back at the bathroom. Hopefully Bess or George had called the police by now and they were on their way.

With a deep breath, I pressed forward. "You pulled off a good trick, Hugo, and for a while there I bought the illusion, just like the police and everyone else."

He frowned but didn't speak. Out of the corner of my eye, I saw Bess, George, and Sawyer slip out of the bathroom and into the back of the room.

"I've learned that there are several kinds of magic," I said. "Drake does illusion, so you created a robbery that obviously fit within that type. The video with the darts gave the illusion that coming to River Heights was a coincidence. It wasn't. You somehow knew that Candy Corlean stored millions of dollars of loose gems at the shop and that the ones you stole would be easiest to take."

I continued. "Using gum to clog locks so that they don't completely close is a classic illusionist move. So you left gum on the floor of the jewelry store. It's also well known that video is often used in illusion." George had told me that.

"But the truth is, you used escape magic to actually open the locks and the gem cabinet. You just made it *look* like an illusion in order to frame Lonestar, who is a known illusionist." George and Bess moved closer to me, leaving Sawyer near the door. "And then there was the trick at the courthouse."

When Drake rattled the handcuffs in the judge's chambers, he was silently telling me I was searching for a thief who was an expert at escapes.

"You never meant for the box to end up in the evidence locker," I said.

Bess caught on. "Oh! You kept the gems you wanted, then planted the rest in the mandala box and put it in what you thought was Drake's hotel room. You probably thought it was Drake in the shower. It was John Smallwood!" Bess shook her head. "Imagine your surprise when it turned out he'd been a jewel thief and they confiscated your box. Poor John Smallwood," Bess groaned dramatically. "Serious case of wrong place, wrong time."

"Can I make a guess here?" George asked. "The box belongs to Gritty Grand. Drake wasn't lying when he kept insisting it wasn't his. But you knew that putting the gems there would once again point to Drake as the thief because of his tight relationship with Gritty."

She quickly put in, "A relationship that doesn't look like divorce to me."

Hugo flinched.

"So the box ended up in the evidence locker. You didn't want to lose the jewels, so you used Houdini-type escape magic to break in and out of the room and the courthouse." I didn't know how he got the key, but as George had said about Houdini, I was pretty sure there was one hidden on Hugo somewhere. . . . I instinctively glanced down at the soles of his shoes, nice-looking dress shoes with a small heel. It seemed possible that the heels could have been hollowed out.

It was Bess who said what I was thinking. "In many ways, you are a better magician than Drake Lonestar."

"I know!" Hugo stood and paced the room. "It's true. I can do escape *and* illusion. So why don't I have the big show? Why don't I have the cash? Why didn't I get the girl?"

Hugo was growing angry, and it made me nervous. More than anything, I wished the police would come rushing in just then. I also realized that I hadn't yet persuaded Hugo to actually confess, so I took a deep breath and plodded on.

"All those lies. Drake trusted you to be his friend! You convinced him the lies were to protect him from fans, but really they were so you could steal millions and frame him for it."

Hugo's face flushed, and he pumped his fist. "Listen, I met Gritty first. I was in love with her, but like everyone else, she was dazzled by Drake." He grimaced. "Gritty picked Drake over me, and they married in secret to prevent a lot of celebrity buzz. When I found out, I advised them to get divorced. They believed me when I said it would be best for both of their careers. So they did officially, though for all intents and purposes they still acted and lived as a married couple.

"Drake got everything. The fame. The magic act. The girl." He sighed. "And I ended up with nothing. So I'm going to do whatever it takes to prove to Gritty that I've always been the right man for her! Including getting her all the money she needs." He grunted.

"Way more than Drake could ever give her."

"Hugo, we need to know where the other gems are." I glanced at Sawyer, who was creeping toward the hotel room door. I really hoped he wouldn't just leave us here like this. I wasn't sure I could hold Hugo much longer. "Do you have them with you now?" I asked.

"As a matter of fact, I do." Hugo suddenly seemed fully relaxed. He smiled, sat back down, and crossed his legs. The posture made me again look at his shoes. I wondered . . .

He grinned. He winked. And then a puff of thick, white smoke filled the room. And a moment later, I was facing an empty chair.

Hugo was gone.

CHAPTER SEVENTEEN

A Magician's Secrets

THE NEXT AFTERNOON I WAS LYING ON George's bed, waiting for her to show me the big project she'd been working on all day.

I tried to peek at the screen, but she blocked me, turning the computer slightly. "Not yet, Nancy. You'll ruin the illusion!"

"Just like Sawyer ruined Hugo's?" I asked with a satisfied smile.

As it turned out, magician Sawyer saw things in Drake Lonestar's hotel room that I'd missed.

When I'd knocked over the bathroom trash can,

I hadn't understood the meaning of the items that spilled out. The bits of wood I'd seen were matchsticks with the heads cut off, and the sugar packets, well, those weren't used for coffee. Both were among the ingredients commonly used to make a magician's smoke bomb.

Sawyer's experience in the River Heights Magic Club told him exactly what Hugo was up to, and he prepared for it.

The only possible exits out of that room were the hole in the bathroom ceiling, the balcony, and the front door. Sawyer had replaced the ceiling tiles when they left the bathroom. The balcony was a harrowing thirteen floors up. That left the door as the only viable escape, so Sawyer decided to position himself there. I'd seen him scooting that way but hadn't even thought to wonder why.

When the smoke bomb went off, he blocked the door to keep Hugo from leaving. Of course he wasn't really a match for beefy Hugo, but the swarms of reporters in the hallway had closed in on him. The police arrived just in time (I was right about my friends calling them), and found the gemstones were hidden in Hugo's shoes.

"Did you finish the video yet, George?" Bess asked as she walked into the room. She was carrying a stack of magazines.

"Almost," George said. She looked up from her computer. "What's with the mags?"

Bess groaned. "Reporters can be so gullible." She waved the pile around in the air. "Every single one of these reported that Gritty Grand had a relationship with Hal Thomas without even questioning it." She sat down next to me.

"Hal's not totally innocent. The publicity was good for him, too," I said. "The controversy of dating a much older woman gets people talking."

"He still uses too much hair gel, if you ask me." George laughed as her fingers flew over the keys. "Nearly done," she murmured.

"So I think I figured out how Hugo got the keys to the jewelry store," I told my friends.

"Really?" George asked.

"Remember when we saw him at the Riverview? He was carrying a coffee cup from the River Run Coffee Shop."

When they both nodded, I went on. "And Candy said she went there on her regular work breaks."

"Ten, noon, and three," Bess recalled.

"She was predictable. And he was a magician. I bet he pickpocketed her while she stood in line and made wax molds of her keys like Houdini."

"But she said she'd never seen him when we showed her his picture," George said.

"All that means is that she didn't *notice* him," I answered. "Hugo was a savvy magician—he was a master at going undetected."

"I'm done," George suddenly announced. "Come see!"

We all gathered around the computer. George was about to push the play button when Ned arrived. "Hello, ladies. What's going on?"

"I'm showing Nancy and Bess a magic trick," George explained. "And I think I figured out the secret to Drake's disappearing courthouse show. All I'll say is that I believe it involves clever use of video."

"Oh, I want to see!" Ned moved in closer to the small screen.

On the screen was an image of River Heights High School. The music George had chosen was the school band. Suddenly the music stopped and the screen went black.

"Now you see it," George said, "now you don't." The screen came back and now, where the high school was stood an amusement park. There was a Ferris wheel where the cafeteria used to be and a carousel in the open area where the gym stood.

"Okay, so the magic needs some work...," George said. "But I think I'm onto something. I just need to figure out how to make it a little less obvious."

"Keep working on it," I said. At this point, I was fine with not completely understanding how the courthouse had disappeared.

Ned chuckled.

"I'm glad you're here," I said, turning to him. I

thought he'd be busy all day finishing reports for my dad and then escorting Smallwood to the airport.

"It turns out that Smallwood is going to hang around for a few more days to get to know Candy better," he said, raising his eyebrows. "So I got the rest of the afternoon off. Turns out I can go to my cousin's fifth birthday party tonight after all." He grinned. "Cake, balloon animals, face painting . . . want to come?"

"How can I say no?" I said with a big laugh as I grabbed my purse and followed Ned out the door.

There was a magician at the party.

Not just any magician, but Sawyer. Turns out that this was the Stupendous Sawyer's first professional gig.

Standing in front of a group of captivated kids, Sawyer performed card tricks and pulled a bunny out of a hat. For his grand finale, he asked for an assistant and chose me out of the crowd.

I boldly climbed into a long box and let my newest friend saw me in half.

The kids cheered when Sawyer said, "Abracadabra" and I stepped out of the box whole again.

"So, Nancy Drew, how's it all done?" Ned asked me as we sat in a back corner of the yard, eating the most delicious lemon cake I'd ever tasted. "Tell me the secret."

I laughed, then shrugged. "Who knows? Magic is a mystery that doesn't need solving."

Dear Diary,

I GUESS HUGO WAS A BETTER MAGICIAN than anyone could have seen . . . even Lonestar! I can't help feeling bad that Lonestar's most trusted adviser ended up betraying him. It can't be easy to be a celebrity in the spotlight like that. There's one thing I know for sure, though: True-blue friends like Bess and George are even more precious than the flawless jewels Hugo tried to steal.

READ WHAT HAPPENS IN THE NEXT MYSTERY

IN THE NANCY DREW DIARIES,

The Clue at Black Creek Farm

"I'M JUST SAYING," MY FRIEND BESS MARVIN said as we pushed open the door of the River Heights Community Center, "I don't see how you can get this excited about vegetables."

She was talking to George Fayne, her cousin and my other best friend, who was following behind with an expression like she'd just sucked on a lemon. Ned Nickerson, my boyfriend, was right behind George, wearing an amused expression.

"They're not just vegetables," George said, in the frustrated tone of someone who'd been arguing with the same person nearly since birth, "they're organic, sustainable, locally grown vegetables. And fruits, too!"

"I just think it's all a little silly," said Bess, sighing as we entered the community center gymnasium, which was set up like a banquet hall, filled with round tables covered with red tablecloths and enticing combinations of fresh harvest produce. A banner welcomed us to the FIRST ANNUAL BLACK CREEK FARM CSA BANQUET AND HARVEST CELEBRATION.

George glared at her cousin. "How is organic farming silly?" she demanded.

Ned adjusted his glasses and spoke up. "I might see what Bess is getting at," he said, giving George a disarming grin. "Not that any farming is silly, but . . . you know, scientists have been trying for years to prove that organically grown produce is better for you, and they've found very little evidence."

George let out a scoff. "Well, thank you, Dr. Science."

I held up my hands in the gesture for truce. "All right, all right," I said.

I was saved from further arguing by the interruption of a grinning blonde woman with a purple streak in her hair.

"OMG, Bess, and George!" the woman cried, appearing out of nowhere to pull the two cousins into a big hug. "The last time I saw you, you were kids; now you're young ladies, as my grandmother would say!"

George and Bess exchanged glances and smiled as the woman slowly let them go.

"Holly," George said, "we're so excited that you invited us to this!" She paused to introduce Ned and me to Holly. "Guys, this is Holly Sinclair. She was Bess's and my awesome Girl Scout leader."

Holly shook each of our hands excitedly. "You guys, I'm so happy you could come!" she said, her cheeks flushed. "Black Creek Farm CSA is doing some really good work, trying to change the way our food gets grown," she said seriously. "They just need some more support from the community. So I convinced them to throw this dinner so people can taste their food!"

"Holly, I told you," Bess said teasingly, "I like organic farms and all, but we're not exactly the culinary decision-makers in our families. And my mom really likes the Stop-N-Go," she added. "Especially since they put in that Starbucks."

Holly shook her head, her dark eyes shining. "Your mom probably wouldn't like it so much if she knew where all that mass-produced food was coming from, or what it's doing to the environment," she said. "Come on, guys, have a seat with me."

Holly led our small group to a nearby table, where we all pulled out chairs.

"Soooo," Holly began, sliding into a seat next to George, "you guys must know that the produce you buy in a grocery store isn't all from around here, right?"

Ned nodded. "Of course," he said. "But that goes without saying. Not every climate will be able to produce every fruit or vegetable there's demand for."

"That's true," Holly said, "but do you think people really think about where their food comes from when it's so shiny and easy to buy at the supermarket? Maybe that orange was picked before it was ripe and flown in on a cargo jet, or else trucked around the country using tons of fossil fuels and releasing all kinds of toxins into the environment. But if people stopped and thought about eating locally, maybe they'd select an apple that was grown down the road—perfectly ripe and much easier to transport."

Ned sighed. "Right," he said.

"Local food usually tastes better too," George pointed out, "because local farmers don't pick their produce until it's perfectly ripe. Produce that's trucked in has to be picked weeks before it's ready, and that affects the flavor."

Holly smiled at her. "Exactly," she said. "And we haven't even touched on organic versus conventional produce, and how many toxins are released into the ecosystem by conventional fertilizers and pesticides."

Ned spoke up. "But scientists haven't found much of a nutritional difference in organic and conventionally grown food," he said.

Holly shrugged. "That's true," she agreed, "but we

don't have to look very hard to find the damage that conventional farming does to the environment."

Bess sighed, shaking her head. "Even if I can see the logic in what you're saying," she said, "I don't do the grocery shopping, Holly. My dad does it, and he's big on bargains."

Holly nodded slowly. "Bess, all I ask is that you listen to the presentation tonight and if you're impressed, if you like the quality of the food we serve, you mention us to your dad. Or pass on some flyers I'd be happy to give you." Holly turned from Bess to look at George, Ned, and me. "That goes for all of you," she said.

I glanced from George to Ned. George was nodding enthusiastically, and even skeptical Ned gave Holly a small smile. "Fair enough," he said.

"Sure," I agreed. While I didn't always eat organic, I definitely believed in being environmentally responsible. And everything Holly had said made sense.

"Oh, look!" Holly pointed behind my head at a tall, gray haired and bearded man. She stood up and waved, and the man turned to her and nodded. "That's Sam Heyworth, the man of the hour."

"Who?" asked Ned.

Holly smiled. "Sam's the founder and owner of the Black Creek Organic Farm and CSA."

"So what is a CSA, exactly?" I asked. The term was familiar, but I wasn't totally sure what it meant.

Holly's eyes sparkled. "I'm so glad you asked! CSA stands for Community Supported Agriculture. Do you know how a CSA works?"

I shook my head.

"It's basically a way to help keep small farms in business, and help people who live in the suburbs get access to fresh, local, in-season produce," she explained. "If your family joined, for example, Nancy, they would pay an upfront fee for the whole growing season—June through November. And every week during that season—or every other week if you bought a half share— you'd come to this community center to pick up the freshest, most in-season veggies and fruits that grew on the farm that week."

I raised my eyebrows. "Picked that week?" I asked. "That's pretty fresh."

Holly nodded. "Right off the farm, my friend. It's as fresh as it gets."

I glanced up to see the bearded man Holly had identified as Sam Heyworth headed our way, followed by a woman about his age with short blonde hair. Holly looked up at them and smiled.

"Sam can tell you everything you want to know about the CSA," she said cheerfully. "Black Creek Farm means a lot to him, doesn't it, Sam?"

Sam walked up to the table and smiled down at Holly. "You know it does," he said, looking around at my friends and me. "Hello. Friends of Holly's, I assume?"

George grinned, her eyes twinkling. "Holly was our Girl Scout leader," she said. "She won't stop talking about your farm and CSA."

Sam chuckled. "Well, I'm flattered," he said. "Running Black Creek Farm is a dream of mine. I gave up a partnership at my law firm to build it."

Ned raised an eyebrow. "So you were a lawyer, and now you're a farmer?" he asked.

Sam nodded. "And I was a stressed-out, unhappy man, frankly, but now I'm . . ." He stopped and turned to look at the blonde woman, who'd come to a stop beside him. ". . . very content," he finished. "Ladies and gentleman, allow me to introduce my wife, Abby. She's given up a lot to support me in pursuing this dream."

The woman turned to my friends and me with a smile, her eyes crinkling at the corners. "Hello, everyone," she said. "I hope you're hungry!"

"We're starving," Bess promised.

Abby and Sam laughed. Sam glanced up, catching the eye of a thirtysomething man with short brown hair and boxy black glasses. He raised his hand, waving the man over. The man nodded, then gestured for a woman with long red hair and a protruding, pregnant belly to follow him.

"This is our son, Jack, and his wife, Julie," Abby explained. "They're from Chicago, but they've been visiting us while they house-hunt in the area."

"Hi," said Jack, stopping a few feet away and looking from face to face with a quizzical look.

Julie stopped right behind him. "Hi, everyone," she said. Now that she was closer, I could see that she looked a little pale. "Oh, gosh, I need to sit down."

Jack looked at her with concern. "Go have a seat!" he said urgently. "In fact, go grab something to eat in the kitchen."

Sam nodded. "That's right, dear," he said. "You're eating for two, remember."

Julie shot a small smile at my friends and me. "Sorry to be rude," she said, "but I think I might take Sam up on that. I've been so hungry lately!"

"When are you due?" Bess asked warmly.

"One more month," Julie said, patting her round belly.

She waved and walked toward the kitchen. I followed her with my eyes, and was surprised when I heard harsh voices coming from nearby.

". . . should've planned for her to eat first," Jack was saying to his father, a sharp edge in his voice. "She's eight months pregnant!"

Sam looked hurt. "And nobody minds her sitting down, or eating early."

"Are you sure?" Jack asked in a lower voice, sneering. "You don't want us out here shaking hands to sell your stupid vegetables?"

Sam's face drooped even further. Abby shot Jack a warning look. "Now, Jack. . . ."

Holly cleared her throat. She was staring straight ahead and I couldn't tell whether she'd heard the argument and was ignoring it, or had really missed the whole thing.